A Cowgirl's Secret

LAURA MARIE ALTOM

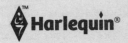 Harlequin®

TORONTO NEW YORK LONDON
AMSTERDAM PARIS SYDNEY HAMBURG
STOCKHOLM ATHENS TOKYO MILAN MADRID
PRAGUE WARSAW BUDAPEST AUCKLAND

Recycling programs
for this product may
not exist in your area.

ISBN-13: 978-0-373-75363-5

A COWGIRL'S SECRET

ABOUT THE AUTHOR

After college (Go, Hogs!), bestselling, award-winning author Laura Marie Altom did a brief stint as an interior designer before becoming a stay-at-home mom to boy-girl twins and a bonus son. Always an avid romance reader, she knew it was time to try her hand at writing when she found herself replotting the afternoon soaps.

When not immersed in her next story, Laura teaches art at a local middle school. In her free time, she beats her kids at video games, tackles Mount Laundry and of course reads romance!

Laura loves hearing from readers at either P.O. Box 2074, Tulsa, OK 74101, or by email at BaliPalm@aol.com.

Love winning fun stuff? Check out www.lauramariealtom.com!

Books by Laura Marie Altom

HARLEQUIN AMERICAN ROMANCE

Don't miss any of our special offers. Write to us at the following address for information on our newest releases.

Harlequin Reader Service
U.S.: 3010 Walden Ave., P.O. Box 1325, Buffalo, NY 14269
Canadian: P.O. Box 609, Fort Erie, Ont. L2A 5X3

This story is for anyone who's suffered molestation. My wish for you is to find the strength to overcome the pain, creating a wondrous life that far exceeds your every dream.

Chapter One

Would it be her?

The closed red door taunted Luke Montgomery. Told him that after nearly ten years searching, the likelihood of Julie Smith actually being Daisy Buckhorn, welcoming him into her home, was nil.

Sleek and sophisticated, the San Francisco building filled with pricey lofts had been a challenge just to enter. Assuming the uniformed doorman wouldn't like unannounced guests, Luke had waited for a distraction before slipping into the stairwell. Four flights later and here he stood, palms sweating just as they had on prom night too many years ago.

Damn Dallas Buckhorn for asking him to perform this task for the family. Dallas hadn't wanted to upset his mother with what could be another fruitless lead. And Luke couldn't say no to his best friend.

Forcing a breath, Luke rapped on the cool, enameled surface, willing his pulse to slow.

Regardless of who answered, he had nothing at stake.

Even if by miracle Daisy did greet him with a warm

smile, for what she'd done—vanishing with nothing more than a cryptic note—he'd long since stopped worrying for her safety, raging at her audacity or crying over his pain. Indifference had become second nature to Luke.

He raised his hand to knock again when the door opened, and there she stood. Ten years older. Steal-your-breath gorgeous. Expression morphing from shock to pleasure to fear, she visibly trembled. Her green eyes pooled with tears. She clutched her white robe tight at the throat. "Oh, my God…Luke?"

"Surprise," he said in a deadpan tone.

In typical Daisy defiance, she raised her chin.

"Do you have any idea what your abrupt exit did to your mom and brothers?"

"They're all fine," she argued. "The web makes it easy enough to check in."

"Then why haven't you—*checked in?* For pity's sake, Daisy, you couldn't even be bothered to attend your own father's funeral?"

"Could we please not do this here?" she asked, her gaze darting up and down the empty hall.

"Is that an invitation?"

"Take it how you want." She left him standing in the doorway in favor of curling up on a white sectional, tugging a red blanket over her legs. On a chrome-and-glass coffee table were a half-dozen wadded tissues, an empty carton of orange sherbet and a pile of manila folders.

Closing the door behind him, Luke cautiously, almost reverently, entered her space. The soaring ceiling allowed for massive windows overlooking a Golden Gate view. Cherry floors warmed otherwise stark furnishings. Alongside a plasma-screen TV stood an Xbox 360 and a haphazard pile of games he wouldn't have guessed her to be playing. "You've done well for yourself."

She shrugged. "Most days I'd agree."

"And others?" He sat in a white leather armchair opposite her.

"Regardless of what you might think, I—" She sneezed.

"Bless you."

Shoulders sagging, for a split second she showed vulnerability. "Thanks."

"You all right?" Leaning forward, resting his elbows on his knees, he noted her flushed complexion.

Nodding, she said, "It's just a cold. I should be at work, but my boss sent me home."

"Nice."

"Greedy," she said with a wry smile. "We've got a killer court date approaching and Barb wants me in top form."

Hands clasped, he nodded. "Understandable." He cut the awkward silence by asking what was foremost on his mind—aside from why she'd ever left. "So… By power of deduction, I'm guessing you're an attorney and the pristine state of this place tells me no kids. How about a husband?"

"Right on all counts."

Why, he couldn't say, but Daisy's answer left Luke shaky with relief. There would never be another chance for them, but in the same respect, the teenage boy in him didn't want her with anyone else.

She asked, "You still horse-whispering?"

He nodded.

Muted traffic noise from five stories below filled a vacuum of discomfort.

"Look…" she said.

"Look…" he said.

After sharing nervous laughs, Luke said, "Ladies first."

She forced a breath, which led to a coughing fit.

"Still like tea with honey?"

Coughing, she nodded. "But I've spent so much time at work, I don't have either."

"Figures," he said under his breath, already headed for the door. "Stay put, *Julie Smith*. I'll be right back."

ONCE LUKE LEFT THE LOFT, every bone in Daisy's body screamed for her to run, but the sad truth was that she lacked the energy—physically, but most especially, emotionally. Ten years' hiding had taken a toll. With Kolt safely at day camp, and then soccer and then sharing dinner with his best friend, now seemed as good a time as any to deal with the truth.

At least part of it.

The entirety, Daisy feared, she might never be ready to tackle. Which was why for now, she gathered a few of her son's stray adventure books, action figures and clothes, placing them in his room, before closing his bedroom door.

She showered then dressed in black yoga pants and a green T-shirt from her law firm's softball team. She blew-dry her long hair. All of the actions were ordinary enough, yet her limbs felt heavy and drugged. Beyond cold symptoms, secrets that had haunted her for far too long clung to her shoulders. On how many New Year's Eves had she promised herself to face her fears? To once and for all not only reunite with her family, but tell the uncensored truth of why she'd left.

Outside, July fog had settled over the usually expansive view, cocooning her in a false sense of security. Of all of the people who'd come in and out of her life, Luke had meant the most. He'd been hardest to leave and stood to be hurt most by her revelations.

While she stood staring out at the grayness, the loft door opened behind her. Luke had long ago imprinted himself upon her soul. So much so that even now, she knew the strong cadence of his walk without turning around.

"I grabbed Popsicles, tea, honey, lemons and chicken-soup fixings. Park your behind on the sofa and I'll get down to the business of nursing you."

"Why are you doing this?" Facing him, she rubbed her hands up her bare arms to ward off a sudden chill. "I know I hurt you—deeply—yet there you stand, loading my freezer with treats and acting as if you don't have a million questions."

"First, fixing is what I do for a living. Second, I figure when you're ready, you'll talk. Until then—" he rummaged beneath her kitchen island, found a saucepan then filled it with water "—might as well give myself something to do."

For as long as she could remember, Daisy had wanted to escape her hometown of Weed Gulch, Oklahoma.

Luke, however, loved nothing more than the solace of wind-swayed prairie grasses. When she'd known him, he'd been more comfortable in the company of horses and dogs than people. Was he still the same?

"Thank you. For the groceries, I mean. And cooking."

"Sure." He lit the gas burner beneath her tea water.

Sitting on a stool at the granite bar, she asked, "How did you find me?"

"Didn't." He took a mug from the cabinet alongside the sink. "Your mom's had a P.I. on retainer ever since you left. When your dad died, she put the matter in Dallas's hands. Most leads he handles, but this one, he didn't have time for. Asked me to handle it."

It. As if all she'd become to her family was an imposition. An obligation they felt honor-bound to see through. Could she blame them? As an eighteen-year-old with the entirety of her trust fund at her disposal, the only thing that'd mattered was getting the hell out of Dodge with her sanity intact. In retrospect, maybe she should've done things differently. What was that old saying?

If foresight was as good as hindsight, we'd be better off by a damned sight.

"Drink."

Daisy looked up to find Luke bearing a fragrant cup of tea. She took a cautious sip of the steaming brew, relishing the soothing honey on her raw throat. "Delicious. I can't remember the last time I've had this."

Leaning against the counter, crossing his jeans-clad legs at the ankles, he snorted. "Used to be you never slowed long enough to be trusted with hot liquids. I remember you as a wild thing. Driven by some unseen force I never understood."

True.

Extensive counseling had long since quieted internal screams. But what happened now? She'd lived under the assumption that she'd never again need to deal with the devil. She missed her mother. Her brothers. But once they heard the truth of why she'd left, would they even want to see her? Or would they blame her for what that monster had done?

"Not gonna lie," Luke said, starting on the soup by filling a Dutch oven with water. "Dallas is expecting my call. I'm supposed to tell him you're found. If you'd like, I can also tell him you'd prefer to remain lost."

"Is that what I am to you?" Wrapping cold fingers around the warm mug, she searched for the right way to explain that only after she'd left Weed Gulch had she felt even a fraction of sanity. "Just some lost soul, wandering? Looking for a home? Because if that is what you think, you're wrong. I've clawed my way out of hell to forge a great life, and—"

"Cut the theatrics. Buckhorn Ranch has every conceivable luxury. I'd hardly equate it with hell."

Shifting on the stool, she snapped, "That's because you don't know what I went through."

"So tell me. What are we talking? A few adolescent fights with your mom? Having to do chores? Homework?" Removing the whole chicken from the package, he rinsed it under running water. "Wish I could say I feel sorry for you, but nothing justifies the pain you've caused your family for the past ten years. *Nothing.*"

He'd commandeered her cutting board and a knife. If he chopped any harder on the carrots for the soup, he'd slice through the counter.

Forcing a breath, she hopped off the stool, rounding the bar to pause alongside him, placing her hand over his. Ignoring the instant jolt of awareness that after all those years was apparently alive and well, she said, "Please stop."

"I can't. I'm so freakin' pissed." Chop, chop, chop. "Putting aside the hurt you caused your mom, what about me, Daisy? Do you have any idea how many nights I stared at my ceiling? Wondering if you were even alive—and if so, what horrible things might've happened to you?"

Throat aching from the effort of holding back tears, she managed to whisper, "That's what I need to explain." She cleared her throat. "What you—no one— understands is that right there in the supposed safety of my home, I lived out the sometimes daily nightmare of those *things*. The kinds of issues no one wants to talk about, or if they do, it's only in shocked whispers."

Putting down the knife to face her, he said, "You're scaring me. What the hell happened that was so bad you couldn't even share the burden with me?"

"I was—" Her mouth went dry as summer sun-scorched Buckhorn Ranch land. She tried speaking, but the words wouldn't come. She'd told her therapist about it. Her boss and best friend, Barb. Even a few of her old sorority sisters knew. So why couldn't she tell the one man she'd ever truly loved?

Pulse racing, she struggled past waves of fear.

Ten years later, Daisy still deeply cared what Luke thought of her. It didn't matter that *Julie Smith* had been named one of San Francisco's top ten young attorneys. *Julie* having graduated with honors didn't do a thing for Daisy, either. *Julie* owned this fabulous loft. *Julie* lived a charmed life. *Julie* was an amazing mother to her son. Poor little Daisy Buckhorn had been gone for a long, long time and that was just the way *Julie* liked it.

Abandoning his busywork, Luke locked his gaze with hers before taking her by the hand, guiding her toward the couch.

"You're burning up with fever," he noted once they'd both sat down. "From just touching your hand it's easy enough to tell. As soon as you spill this apparent deep, dark secret, I want you to take a couple of ibuprofen and go to bed."

She nodded.

Repositioning, he winced before pulling an action figure out from beneath him. Holding it up for inspection, he asked, "Closet toy fanatic?" His stab at lightening the mood proved an epic failure. Tears stung her eyes again.

Squeezing her fingers, he urged, "Come on. There's not a thing you could tell me I won't be able to handle."

Daisy longed for Luke's reaction to her secret to be swift and wholly in her favor. She wanted outrage to send him jumping up from the sofa to return to Weed Gulch that second to beat the old coot black and blue. That's what she wanted, but since no words escaped her tight throat, she, instead, sat ramrod-straight, deathly still save for clenching her hands.

"Well?" he urged. "Now's as good a time as any to say something—anything—to convince me you had a plausible reason to almost destroy every soul who's ever loved you."

Tears fell, but though her cheeks were damp, her dry mouth refused to speak.

"I don't owe you squat, but unlike you, I'm going to at least have the decency to tell you up front that all the tears in the world aren't going to change my mind. Putting my feelings aside, your leaving damn near killed your mother. Who knows, maybe it even contributed to your daddy's death. You've got a lot of nerve—"

"Stop!" Not knowing what she'd survived, he had no right to make such hurtful claims. Taking a tissue from the coffee table to dab her eyes and cheeks, she summoned the same strength that'd gotten her this far and pointed toward the door. "Get out. Report to Dallas I'm alive and well and thank him for his concern, but no matter how much I miss all of my family and friends, I'm never going back."

His jaw hard, Luke stood. The cold stare he leveled at her chilled her to her core.

Tell him! her conscience screamed.

Tell him how everyone's favorite ranch hand, the kind and lovable family friend, Henry Pohl, had molested her nine ways to Sunday. Don't leave out the parts where he'd threatened to kill her family if she told, or how the abuse had been a daily occurrence until she'd been strong enough to fight him off physically.

"If that's how you feel," Luke said, not a trace of compassion in his words, "far be it from me to force you to do the right thing. If you're able to live with the consequences of what you've done, knowing how many nights your mom still cries herself to sleep, then by all means—" he strode to the kitchen, taking his hat from the counter to slap it on his head "—carry on with this madness of yours till it chokes you."

"Luke, wait," she called when he opened the door and stepped into the hall. Why, she couldn't say, but she couldn't let him leave like this—angry and blaming her when Henry was the real villain in this story.

When Luke kept right on walking toward the elevator, she followed. "There's so much you don't understand. Stay and maybe—"

The elevator signaled its arrival with an elegant ding.

Off stepped a feverish-looking Kolt, followed by his best friend's mom.

"Hey," Heidi said, an arm around Kolt's sagging shoulders. "Knowing you're sick, too, the hall is the last place I expected to find you."

"Um, yeah," Daisy said, biting hard enough on her bottom lip to draw blood. *Get on the elevator, Luke. If I can't handle telling you about Henry, there's no way I'm able to introduce you to your son.*

Chapter Two

Craving closure when he feared there was none, Luke drummed his fingers on a narrow black table holding white lilies with an overpowering scent.

"Th-thanks for bringing him home," Daisy said to a brunette soccer-mom type and a kid.

Luke froze. *Home?* Since when did Daisy have a kid?

"Mom," the boy mumbled, hugging her waist, "I threw up at practice."

"I'm sorry." Skimming her hand over his head with a tenderness she'd never had for Luke, Daisy said, "Heidi, I can't thank you enough for bringing him home."

"No problem," Heidi said, glancing from Daisy to Luke. "Everything all right?"

"Fine." Daisy hugged the boy to her. When she turned toward her loft, the color had long since drained from her face. "I—I've got to go."

"Sure," her friend said. "But while I'm here, Toby lost this week's craft supply list. Mind if I copy Kolt's? I'm afraid if I ask their teacher again she's going to land both of us in day camp detention."

Pouring on the speed, Daisy said, "I'm not sure where Kolt's is. When I find it, I'll call."

"Slow down," the boy complained. "You're gonna make me pukc again."

Glancing over her shoulder to Luke, as he followed them, Daisy's friend asked, "Are you sure you're all right? I didn't interrupt, did I?"

"Not at all," Daisy assured, practically shoving the boy into her loft.

"Ouch!" he complained. "Mom, you're hurting mc."

"I feel like I stepped into the middle of something. Want me to watch Kolt?" Eyeing Luke, Daisy's friend said under her breath, "You know, in case you two need to talk."

It was on the tip of Luke's tongue to admit just how weary he'd grown of even being in the same space as Daisy until the dark-haired boy glanced at him through eyes matching his own.

Dawning, slow and building, spread through Luke, igniting both wonder and fury. No wonder Daisy was acting so skittish. For the past ten years, she'd hidden his son.

Luke snagged her by her upper arm, not caring he'd caused her to wince. "We'd really appreciate you watching Kolt, wouldn't we, Julie?"

"Y-yes, please," she said. "Heidi, if you need me, we'll just be down the hall."

"Mom?" the boy—Luke's son—asked. "Need help?"

"No, thank you." Wearing a smile Luke knew from experience to be fake, Daisy said, "This will only take a second and then we'll watch a movie."

With their audience safely behind the loft's closed door, Luke dragged Daisy to the seating area in front of the elevator. "Talk."

She shook her head.

"Damn you," he ground out in a low tone, trying to keep it together if for no other reason than the last thing he needed was a nosy neighbor butting into a conversation ten years in the making. "Let me guess," he said upon releasing her to push her into an armchair. "Your deep, dark secret you just couldn't bear for anyone to know was that you were pregnant with our son?"

Swallowing hard, she nodded.

"You're such a coward, you caused your family— *me*—years of worry and pain just to hide a teen baby?"

"Th-there's more to it than that."

Pacing, hands to his temples, Luke wasn't sure whether to punch the nearest wall or hightail it to Daisy's loft, taking back the son she'd hidden from him apparently without so much as a shred of remorse. His rational side knew the last thing their child needed was to learn he had a father in a traumatizing way. Because of that, he settled for asking, "If Dallas's P.I. hadn't found you, were you ever planning to tell me?"

"Yes."

"Lord…" Hand to his forehead, he slowly backed away. The damned cloying flowers made him want to retch. "I can't believe this."

"I'm sorry. I really was going to tell you. I just—it never seemed like the right time." The more she wrung her hands, the more he fought the urge to wring her elegant neck.

"I've imagined hundreds of possible reasons for you taking off like you did—vanishing without so much as a written apology. I thought you'd been kidnapped or had amnesia. Never for one second did I believe you'd voluntarily abandon me—your whole life. But this…" He shook his head. "You're lower than low. Knowing you carried my son inside you wouldn't have been bad news to me but the ultimate blessing. What did I ever do to deserve this?"

"Nothing," she said through tears for which he had no sympathy. "I—I thought it better for everyone if I stayed away."

"Do you have any idea what you've done? What an absolute train wreck you've made of not only my life, but our son's? Can you even imagine the questions he's going to have? Did you tell him I was dead? Or did you just not care? How am I ever going to earn the trust of a ten-year-old who never even knew I existed?"

Hands on her hips, raising her chin, Daisy snapped, "If you don't want him, go back to Weed Gulch."

"Wouldn't you just love that?" His tone dripped with sarcasm. "No doubt nothing would make you happier."

"That's ridiculous. Now that you're here, I'm relieved. If I'd truly wanted to keep Kolt from you the rest of his life, I could've done it."

"That's supposed to make me feel better?" He shot her a look of such pure, raw disgust, Daisy felt physically assaulted.

She doubled over. Sobs started and wouldn't stop.

If only she'd told him about Henry. Then maybe Luke would understand. As it was, everything had come out all wrong. In a perfect world, she would have explained the nightmare that had caused her to leave before the miracle she'd found in their son.

Luke said, "The gentlemanly thing would be for me to give you a hug and tell you everything's gonna be all right, but you know what, Daisy? That's something I can't do. My whole life I've wanted to be a father. I married not long after you left, hoping to get the chance at a family." His sharp laugh told her what she already knew from having kept up with Weed Gulch gossip online. His marriage had lasted less time than the courtship. "The trust issues you gifted me with took that dream and shot it straight to hell." Lowering his voice, he asked, "Where do I even start developing a relationship with my kid? Does he blame me for not having been in his life? What have you told him about me? Being ten, surely he doesn't think he came from the stork?"

"Mom?" Kolt stepped outside the loft. "I heard shouting."

Heidi followed. "I'm sorry, Julie. I tried keeping him with me, but he ran away."

"It's all right," Daisy said with a sniffle. "If you wouldn't mind, we're going to need privacy." Daisy went to her son.

Luke followed.

"Sure," Heidi said, her wide eyes questioning. "Let me grab my purse."

With her friend gone and her son alongside her, Daisy

wished for courage, but found none. She'd always known this day was coming, though that knowledge did little to make it easier.

Clearing her throat, she suggested, "Why don't we all sit down."

Kolt didn't budge. "Who are you?" he asked Luke. "Why are you making my mom cry?"

"Sorry about that," Luke said, "but she did something that hurt not just me but you. Now, she's sad."

Daisy held Kolt for all she was worth. She had never needed her son more. "Sweetheart, remember how I told you your father lives really far away, and how he loves you bunches, but hasn't been able to see you?"

Her son looked from her to scowling Luke. "Yeah…"

"W-well, I wish this moment could've been more special for you, but sweetie, this man—Luke Montgomery—is your dad."

Luke knelt. "Hey, bud. I, ah, sure am glad to finally meet you."

"If you really are my dad," Kolt said, "then how come you never loved me enough to see me before now?"

"It's complicated." Daisy molded her hands to Kolt's shoulders, hugging him against her.

"I hate that word." Kolt broke free of Daisy's hold. "Why can't you ever just tell me the truth? I know my dad doesn't love me and that's why he never wanted to see me."

"Whoa!" When Kolt took off running toward his room, Luke snagged him back. "You wanna know the truth? Until ten minutes ago, I never knew you existed.

More truth? I'm really mad at your mom for not even telling me she was having my baby."

"Really?" The boy looked from his mother to his father. With each bit of information Kolt's eyes widened and Daisy's heart broke a little more. What had she done? In hopes of protecting her child from that monster, Henry, she'd hidden him away from everyone who would have loved him, in the process, hurting him more than she ever could've known. "Is that true, Mom?"

Eyes pooling, Daisy nodded. "I'm so sorry. I never meant for you to find out this way. I just..." Her advanced degree didn't help impossible words come easily.

"If you give me a chance," Luke said to their son, "nothing would make me happier than getting to know you the way a father should know his son."

"B-but you're a stranger." As if transforming himself into a self-sufficient island, Kolt also wrestled free of his father's hold.

"That's my point. You're my son. We should at least be friends, don't you think?"

Expression more confused than ever, Kolt escaped to his room, slamming his door behind him.

Daisy chased after him, but Luke grabbed her. "Let him be. Poor kid has a lot to digest. In time, he'll be all right."

"How do you know?" Daisy snapped. "Like Kolt said, you're strangers."

"And whose fault is that?" Luke asked.

The line on its own stung. Knowing Daisy had no

one but herself to blame delivered its own special pain. "Regardless, I think you should leave."

"The hell I will." Brushing past her, he parked himself on one of the kitchen-counter bar stools. "Got any beer?"

"I'm serious," she said in a whisper. "Get out. Kolt needs time to adjust, and I need—"

"I don't care what *you* need," Luke said in a dangerous tone. "This is about my son and me. If you'd wanted the idyllic pregnancy announcement, you might have considered staying in Weed Gulch."

Exhausted, no doubt feverish, with an equally sick son on her hands, Daisy wanted to fight back, but lacked the strength, not to mention the justification. When it came to not telling Luke he was a father, Daisy knew herself to be one hundred percent in the wrong. "You may not believe it," she said, "but I am incredibly sorry."

KOLT USUALLY LOVED HIS ROOM. He had lots of great stuff to play with and, since his favorite color was blue, his mom had let him pick out blankets and pillows and even paint the walls a color she said reminded her of an angry sea. He'd never really got what that meant, but since he was never talking to her again, he didn't guess it mattered. Now, his room, and their whole loft, felt like a jail.

Though he couldn't tell what they were saying, he knew whatever was going on between that man and his mom wasn't good.

His mom hadn't lied to him before, but how was Kolt supposed to know that guy really was his dad?

Kolt wanted to get another look at him. Like maybe if he stared long enough, he might feel something. Most of his friends really liked their dads, so maybe Kolt would like his, too. Right now, though, he didn't think so.

Somebody knocked on his door.

"Go away!" Kolt shouted. It was bad enough that he already felt super crappy, now to have all this weird grown-up stuff going on made him feel worse.

His mom opened the door. "I've got medicine and juice."

"I said go away!"

"Kolt…" After setting a glass and two pills on the table by his bed, she sat next to him. "We really need to talk."

He scooted as far away from her as he could without falling onto the floor.

"Okay." She sighed. "Guess I can see how I might have cooties."

"You're so lame." Arms crossed, he informed her, "Cooties are for, like, second-graders. I'm too old for that stuff."

"Right. I forgot." She tried ruffling his hair, but he dodged away before she touched him. Usually, he liked it when they horsed around, but now he wasn't sure what to think. "Would you like to talk more with your dad? He's in the living room and would really enjoy getting to know you."

"Can't you just leave me alone? Why would I want to talk to some guy I don't even know? I don't feel good and I just wanna sleep."

"Sure." Hand to his forehead, she said, "You feel like

you have a little fever, so please chew these for me and then drink your apple juice."

He hated stupid chew-up baby aspirin, but because Kolt wanted his mom to leave him alone, he went ahead and took it. Maybe if he went to sleep, when he woke up his mom and the guy who said he was his dad would be gone.

"How's HE DOING?" Luke asked when Daisy emerged from their son's room, softly closing the door behind her.

"Physically, I'm fairly certain he'll live. As for his emotional state, I've never seen him like this. He's usually a happy kid."

"Give him a break," Luke snapped. "News like this would send anyone over the edge."

"You've officially been his father for what? All of twenty minutes? Where do you get off giving me parenting advice?"

"I'll tell you where—"

"Stop!" Their son stood in the hall with his hands over his ears. "Both of you please shut up!"

Luke found the sight jarring. He'd always loved kids and to now be the cause of his own child's pain was devastating.

"Sorry," Luke said to his son. "The last thing I want is for you to get caught up in our grown-up frustration."

"I don't even know what that means," the boy said. "All I do know is that before you were here, my mom didn't cry and I could sleep without hearing yelling."

As if finding Daisy and learning he was a father

hadn't been enough to digest in a single day, Luke was now faced with the probability that through no fault of his own, his son might never learn even to accept him, let alone actually to enjoy Luke's company.

"I'm going to grab a motel room," Luke said. "Kolt, I didn't mean for you to get caught up in the middle of all of this, and I hope you feel better soon. As for you," he said to Daisy, "give me a time and place that works for you in the morning. We have a lot of details to hammer out."

Out of Kolt's earshot, Daisy gave Luke the name of one of her favorite restaurants on the wharf, agreeing to meet at nine.

When he was gone, the air felt lighter, making it easier to breathe. For the longest time, she leaned against the closed door. In such a short time span, how could so much go wrong? That morning, her only worry had been a sniffle and an insane caseload. Now, her whole world stood on the verge of falling apart.

"What are you doing?"

Daisy glanced up to find her son staring.

"Honestly," she said, busying flighty hands by straightening what was surely disheveled hair, "I'm taking a time-out."

"Why did you lie to me about my dad?"

Her son's question deserved a well-thought-out answer, but she didn't have one. "Come here," she said, hand on his back, leading him to the sofa. "I was really young when I got pregnant with you. I got scared and ran away. After a while I made a new life for you and me, and it seemed easier to forget the past." She took a deep breath. "But I know how selfish that was. Can you forgive me, Kolt?"

Her son stared at her with eyes so much like Luke's. "I guess." He turned away, then added, "He looks like me."

"I've always thought so," Daisy admitted. "So many times I wanted to tell you all of this, but remember when you accidently broke my favorite crystal vase, and were afraid to tell me?"

He nodded.

"That's how I've felt about your father, only on a much bigger scale. When he came here today, I was just as surprised as you. But now that you two know about each other, aren't you curious about what he's like?"

Shrugging, Kolt said, "I guess. Is he always so grouchy?"

A wistful smile tugging her lips, Daisy reminisced, "Luke was always the most kind and gentle person I knew. That's why I loved him. He made everything that scared me seem not so bad."

"Do you still love him?"

What a question. "No. But when we made you, I thought he was the most amazing guy on the planet."

"Eeeuw." He made a face. "Does that mean you *did it* with him?"

Refusing even to respond to a birds-and-bees question from her ten-year-old, Daisy held out her hand. "Come on. Somewhere high up in my closet are pictures I'd like you to see."

Photos Daisy had carefully avoided for so long.

She had a hard enough time dealing with remembered

images of her former life, but in time, those had grown fuzzy. To hold smiling snapshots of all she held dear would be excruciating. Her mom, grinning in her garden. Her favorite brother, Cash, hamming it up with GQ poses. Dallas and her father, the stoic ones of the Buckhorn clan. Never overtly demonstrative, but both with hearts of pure gold. Wyatt, rarely seen without a football or pretty girl. And then there were shots of Luke. Handsome, funny, sweet. His grins took her breath away. His kisses filled her with hope and wonder and dizzying pleasure she hadn't even tried finding again. Why should she, when she deep-down knew such perfection could no longer exist.

Chapter Three

"For the hundredth time, I'm sorry."

Luke glanced over the rim of the black coffee he'd been nursing to see Daisy flash a half smile. It ought to be a crime for a woman to be so gorgeous. Made it damn near impossible for a man to think.

"You wanted to talk," she persisted, "so here I am."

"Not that simple."

Sighing, she said, "This is one of Kolt's favorite places. Look—" She pointed out their tableside window. "See the sea lions? Kolt gets a kick out of watching them."

"I'll bet." What else did their son like to do that Luke had no idea about? He couldn't quite wrap his head around the notion that even though Kolt was his blood, they were strangers with nothing in common. Case in point, something about eating eggs over crashing bay water, high up on a rickety pier had Luke on edge. He was a land man through and through. Yet his son apparently loved the water.

"I thought about bringing him, but he seemed to be feeling so much better that I sent him to day camp.

Besides which," she toyed with the tea tag still hanging from her mug, "the last thing he needs is more arguing. I'd like for us to present a united front."

Slathering butter on a fussy croissant when he'd have preferred a buttermilk biscuit, Luke snorted. "Haven't we already been over the fact that I don't give a damn what you'd like? When it comes to our son, of course, I only want what's best for him and I find it downright insulting you'd imply otherwise. In fact—" His cell rang. Removing it from his back pocket, he checked the number. "Dallas. Want to talk?"

She vigorously shook her head.

"You're going to have to face him sooner or later."

"I prefer later."

Rolling his eyes, he answered, "Hey."

In usual Dallas style, Daisy's brother barked louder than the sea lions. "You actually found her? Is she at that address? If so, Mom and I will be on the next plane out."

"Whoa," Luke said, hating that he was now firmly in the middle of an ungodly mess. "Like I said in my text last night, it's complicated. Daisy's not quite ready for company."

"Company, hell!" Dallas roared loud enough for Daisy to wince. "We're family. We deserve an explanation for what made her sneak off like a two-bit floozy in the night."

"Agreed. But there's a lot going on here I didn't expect to find."

"Like what? Is she married with kids? Our flying out there isn't a problem."

Eyeing Daisy, Luke said, "I'm pretty sure she'd rather come to you."

She nodded.

"She say as much?"

"Yeah." Luke rubbed his whisker-stubbled jaw.

"Wouldn't happen to be with her now, would you?"

"No." Luke hated lying. Always had. Occasionally it was a necessary evil. For Kolt's sake, Luke wanted to ease his boy into meeting the rest of his family. If the entire Buckhorn clan showed up at his front door, it could be overwhelming.

"Planning on seeing her before you head back?"

"Yeah."

"Kindly tell her she has twenty-four hours to get her butt to this ranch, or—"

Daisy snapped, "Give me the phone."

Sure? Luke mouthed.

Ignoring him, she lunged for it. "Dallas Buckhorn, your blow-and-go routine won't work on me. I'm sorry for what I did to all of you—truly, I am. But I'll be back in my own time." She paused to listen, tears pooling her eyes. "I know. Please tell Mom I love her and promise to be home soon." After a few more minutes' conversation, she hung up only to run off to the bathroom.

It took everything Luke had in him not to chase her.

But why should he? The amount of emotional baggage between them could fill this swanky place clear to the rafters.

Sighing, he propped his elbows on the table, staring out at the unnatural view. If God had meant for folks to eat breakfast over water, He'd have given them webbed feet. Still, he supposed the bay was all right to look at in its own sort of way. It seemed restless. Like he felt.

A few minutes later, Daisy returned looking composed.

"All right?" he asked more because of his upbringing than because he cared. His mother had raised him to be a gentleman, and as such, he never could stand to see a woman cry—even if this particular woman had some sorrow coming.

"Good as can be expected," she said with a shrug. "Hearing my brother's voice twisted me up inside. I wasn't prepared for the rush of feelings it brought on. Reminded me how badly I miss my family—even Dallas. He and I were never close."

"Cash speaks of you often." Luke nabbed a piece of bacon. "Mostly about the good times. Misses you something fierce."

"I miss him, too. Maybe because we're closest in age, but he's secretly my favorite."

Luke smiled. "That boy's straight up full of himself."

"Still handsome?"

Just as much as you are pretty. The way a fog had rolled in, softening the sunlight on her hair, tightened his stomach. He hated the part of himself that had never quite gotten over her. "He's all right. But as a man, I'm not really into his type."

"Sure, sure. You don't have to hide your attraction from me." Her unexpected smile was his undoing. Oh—he had an attraction all right, but for the lone female of the Buckhorn siblings.

"All kidding aside, what's your plan? Because if you and I don't reach a peaceable custody agreement, I don't have a problem with it getting ugly. I've already missed ten years with my son and I refuse to miss a minute more."

"I understand." She paled, only this time it had nothing to do with the ever-increasing fog. "I'll need to speak with my boss. Clear my schedule. Also, I think it would be best if initially, I meet up with my family without Kolt. I want them prepared so that meeting him doesn't come as quite such a shock."

"Agreed."

While hammering out more details, it occurred to Luke that Daisy Buckhorn was still to this day the best-looking woman he'd ever seen. Good thing he wasn't in the market for romance. More times than he could count, he'd been burned. He gave his heart too easily, only to have it handed back. Why? Females claimed he was incapable of trust—a fact for which he had Daisy to thank. Ironic, seeing how his job largely depended on him gaining an animal's trust. Too bad for him women and horses didn't have all that much in common.

"I WAS SO SCARED I'd never see you again."

"I'm sorry," Daisy said, hugging her mother while they both cried in the entry hall of the home where she'd grown up. Georgina Buckhorn used the same orange blossom-scented lotion she always had, and, for Daisy, memories of being sweetly tucked into her bed and rocked through every scraped knee were overwhelming. Trembling, she ingested the full burden of what she had done. In escaping Henry, she'd virtually thrown away everyone she'd ever loved. "I didn't mean to hurt you. I didn't know what else to do."

"You should've damn well talked to us," Dallas said, next in line to crush her with a hug. "We're family. There's nothing we couldn't have worked our way through—especially something as blessed as you having Luke's baby."

Daisy prayed that by the time she left Weed Gulch, she'd have found the courage to tell her brother—along with the rest of her family—the true reason she'd run.

"Lord, I missed you," Cash said when it was his turn for a hug. "And damned if you aren't as pretty as I am handsome." The comment was typical Cash and caused a much-needed release of tension.

"Hey, squirt." Wyatt held her tight. "You think just because you're all grown-up you can bust into the Boys' Only tree house, think again." His tears gave him away as being a big softy. Some of her earliest memories were of begging Wyatt to let her into whatever his latest club might be. He'd usually torture her with tickling, only to grant her entry eventually.

On the fringe of her family stood strangers to whom she was now related by marriage. Dallas introduced her to his twins, Bonnie and Betsy. More guilt weighed on Daisy with the realization that she should've been there for Dallas when he'd lost his first love, Bobbie Jo.

"Nice to meet you," Bonnie said. "Did you bring presents?"

"Bonnie!" Dallas scolded.

"It's okay, Daddy," Betsy said, "I wanna know, too."

Daisy laughed through more tears. "I'm sorry, but I forgot your gifts. Next time I'm here though, we'll skip all of this hugging and go straight to opening presents. Deal?"

Bonnie ambushed her with a surprise hug. "I like you."

Returning the child's embrace, missing her son, Daisy said, "I like you, too. Let's be great friends."

"What about me?" Betsy asked.

"You're going to be my great friend, too." Hugging both girls, Daisy couldn't help but hope the girls would also grow close to their cousin, Kolt. He might be older than them, but he was still a little kid at heart.

"And this," Dallas said, his arm around the shoulders of a pretty redhead who held an infant swaddled in pink, "is my wife, Josie, and our daughter, Mabel."

"She's precious," Daisy cooed to the baby. "You, too," she said to her sister-in-law. "I was always so sick of being the only girl. Nice to know I'll now have company."

"Then I hope we'll be friends, too," a brunette said, Cash alongside her with his arm resting low on her hips. "My name's Wren, and we also have a baby. Her name is Robin, but she has a cold so we left her home with her sitter."

"Nice meeting you," Daisy said, overwhelmed by not only how her family had grown, but by the outpouring of affection. Would they still be so welcoming once she told them her news? "I hope your baby feels better soon. Sick kiddos are never fun."

"If you don't mind my asking," Wren probed, "why didn't you bring your son?"

"Um, I wanted his first meeting with all of you to be unfettered. With so much time having passed, I have a lot to discuss that I don't particularly want him to hear." Dallas loved Henry like a second father—as did all of her brothers. There was no telling how they'd react to Daisy's confession. The last thing she wanted was for Kolt to be present when that awful, inevitable conversation finally took place.

"Fair enough," Wren said.

"Who's hungry?" Georgina asked. "I've got enough ham and trimmings ready to be set out on the dining-room table to feed a small army."

"Good thing," Wyatt said, trailing after her. "That's just about how many folks we have."

WITH THE SETTING SUN spilling gold into the ranch home's living room, family all around her and her mother's apple pie still warming her belly, Daisy should've been content. Instead, while her brothers and sisters-in-law helped clean the kitchen, she sat ramrod-straight on the sofa, fidgeting with her only ring. An emerald she'd bought for herself after passing the bar exam. Always having been a huge *Wizard of Oz* fan, the stone reminded her that while there's no place like home, Dorothy had gained her true strength in the journey, not the end result. Daisy had weathered many storms to return her to this place. But she still had a couple to go.

First, she needed to find the courage to expose Henry. Second, she'd return and introduce her son.

Two huge obstacles that at the moment felt insurmountable.

"Your family seems pretty happy about meeting Kolt," Luke said. "I just don't understand why you ran off. Hell, you'd already graduated. It's not like half the kids we went to high school with weren't already headed for the altar." Luke sat next to her, and their thighs brushed, flooding her with awareness. His radiant heat combined with guilt, making her chest ache from the effort to breathe.

Nodding, she said, "I know. And I'd really appreciate you not reminding me every five minutes what an awful person I am."

"For what you've done to me—our son—you've got a lot more than a little chastising to contend with. My family's itching to lash into you. It'll be a good time." His speech ended with a condescending pat to her knee.

She hated him, so why did she feel each of his fingertips scorch through to her skin? She'd underestimated her former feelings for Luke. At a time when her whole world had been falling apart, he'd been her only solid ground. Now, when yet again her life had turned upside down, a long-buried part of her instinctively longed to turn to him for comfort and support—stupid, considering he grabbed every opportunity to bring her down.

You think you don't deserve it?

It didn't seem possible that only a short while earlier,

she'd been a strong, confident woman, yet now her every doubt and insecurity had resurfaced. Each time someone entered the room, she feared facing Henry. Where was he lurking? Yes, keeping Kolt from Luke had been the worst of Daisy's many bad decisions, but if Luke knew her true reason for escaping Weed Gulch, would he be any more sympathetic?

"You don't have to stay," she said quietly, not wanting to wake the twins who'd crashed on the sofa opposite the one she and Luke shared. "In fact, I'm not sure why you chose to come at all."

"Simple. I trust you about as much as my old farm truck that has three hundred thousand miles." Nudging her shoulder, he added with a mean-spirited wink, "Only you've got less body damage."

Rising, she said, "Please, go. This reunion is hard enough, without—"

Also on his feet, meeting her stare from a perilously close position, he whispered, "Good. You stole my heart and then my son. I want you to feel every ounce of the hell you've put me through. I want you to hurt, Daisy Buckhorn. And just when you might feel better, I want to drag you down again."

Why, why, when Luke's speech should have incensed her, did Daisy recognize the scent of his breath? She'd once loved him more than she'd thought it possible to love someone—at least until a maternity-ward nurse had settled Kolt into her arms.

"There aren't enough words to describe how I detest you. How you've built this fabulous life for yourself without so much as a thought for everyone you left behind."

Silent tears streaming down her cheeks, Daisy hugged her arms over her chest. Nodding, she internalized his every critical word, negating years of supposedly successful therapy in mere seconds. Once again she was a little girl, hiding from a monster, begging to a nonexistent God for Henry not to touch her.

"Don't cry," Luke said. "All the tears in the world aren't going to change what I think of you."

"I—I know. And I—I don't blame you for hating me." *I hate myself for ever letting that filthy old man near me.* Most especially she hated still being afraid to share her darkest secret with the sole person she'd always been able to trust.

"I've missed this," Daisy said to her mom Sunday morning while helping her roll out biscuit dough. "I feel like I can never apologize enough." Eyes again filling with tears, she walked into her mother's embrace.

"I'm the one who should be saying sorry. The fact you felt you couldn't come to me when you found out you were pregnant means volumes. As your mother, I should've known."

Daisy had many times felt the same—only about how her mom couldn't have seen the signs of what Henry had done. Daisy immersed herself in every facet of Kolt's life. Where had her mother been when Henry had—no. Daisy was finished questioning the past. What was done was done.

"Please, come home for good," Georgina asked. "I

want to know my daughter. Make up for all of the time we've lost."

"I want that, too," Daisy said. And she did. *Desperately.*

"Wh-when your father died, his last wish was that I find you and heal whatever broke our family apart. Please come home, honey. I know you lead a busy life. I'm proud of the woman you've become. But if only for a short while, could you put all of that on hold to let me in?"

What could she say? Was this when Daisy asked her mother to move to California where Henry couldn't find them? Or, did she take a deep breath and return to Weed Gulch?

"Don't answer right away." Fussing with her biscuit cutter, Georgina wasn't the strong, self-assured woman Daisy remembered. Dark circles under her eyes told of her sleepless nights. Her normally fastidious braid sported escapee hairs on the right side. "In fact, never mind. It was a silly idea. Forget I ever asked."

"No." Daisy snatched a pea-size bite of dough, popping it in her mouth.

"What does that mean?" While placing the biscuits on a baking sheet, Georgina's hands trembled. "You won't consider moving?"

Daisy shook her head and smiled faintly. "I meant your question wasn't silly, and that yes, I will stay with you."

"Really?" Georgina's voice had grown raspy with emotion.

Daisy nodded, holding out her arms for another of

her mom's comforting hugs. Yes, this decision was rash and not even remotely thought out, but she was home. And she wanted to stay—at least for a little while.

"AS MUCH AS I WANT to get on with getting to know my son, do you think this sudden move is wise?" Luke knew he shouldn't have volunteered to make the long drive to Tulsa International Sunday night, but before Daisy returned with Kolt, Luke wanted to clear the air. The last time they'd talked, he'd said some harsh things he wasn't proud of, but the woman made him feel like a grizzly with a thorn stuck in his paw. In the dim light reflecting from the truck's gauges, he couldn't help but notice how exhausted Daisy looked. Apparently the trip had been tougher than she'd let on. "Shouldn't you take at least a month or two to let the idea of returning to Weed Gulch on even a semi-permanent basis sink in?"

"Probably," she admitted, staring out the side window at the purple hues of the sun setting on rolling hills. The outside temperature was still warm enough to make a necessity of keeping the AC blowing steadily. "That said, if I don't do it now, I'll need to wait till Kolt's next school year."

"That's my point," he said with a glance in her direction. "Should you be making a major life decision so fast? Is our son up for the job of meeting all new friends and getting to know his father?"

"I'm sure my therapist would say no. I, however, have fences to mend and time's ticking."

"You keep saying, *I*. Have you put any thought into how Kolt's going to take this?"

"Of course," she snapped. "At first, it will be hard, but surrounded by family and horses and fresh air, he'll learn to love Weed Gulch."

"As much as you? Need I remind you of the not-so-small fact that you couldn't wait even long enough to tell me goodbye before you got the hell out of our one-horse town?"

"I had my reasons."

Luke snorted.

The woman was certifiable. Though the rock in his gut told him Daisy still had secrets causing the shadows beneath her eyes, he had to admit he couldn't wait to start hanging out with their son.

Chapter Four

"For the record," Barb said Monday morning, "I think this is a perfectly dreadful idea."

"Duly noted." Regardless, Daisy continued unloading her office-desk drawers into boxes. From the Remold Building's twenty-second floor, the city view was surreal. The furnishings were sleek chrome, glass and rich leather. Their corporate clients expected the best and didn't mind shelling out the big bucks required to obtain it.

Standing at just over five foot ten, Barb was a big, brassy redhead who hot-rolled her hair daily into a helmet of curls. Her clothes were all custom and her jewelry bodyguard-worthy. In court, her opponents nicknamed her Barbwire for her cutting legal mind. Outside of her workday, her heart was as big as her wallet. "Not only does your leaving put me in a major bind with the Hallworth case next week, but think about what this is going to do to Kolt. Everything he's ever known is here, in San Francisco. He's a city kid. How's he going to take living in the sticks of Oklahoma?"

"Kolt will be fine."

Barb crossed her arms. "Why don't you take a leave of absence? A year if you need it. But don't do anything rash. Get a short-term tenant in your loft and don't officially give up Kolt's slot at school."

"I get all of your points, but the one thing you forgot to mention is the not-so-small matter of Kolt's father. My son deserves to get to know the man."

Sighing, Barb looked to the ceiling. "You're being melodramatic—not to mention simplistic. You think just because this Luke character made you a cup of tea with honey that he's going to magically forgive you for keeping his son from him for the past ten years?"

"I'd be lying if I said Luke's not upset—understandably so. But I know he'll forgive me, and—"

Barb smacked her palm on the desk. "Spit on the floor and call me Violet, you're nuttier than an Okie fruitcake. This man will never again put his trust in you. Wait a minute… Please tell me you're not harboring a secret reunion fantasy?"

"Of course, not. But I don't want to think of him as an enemy." Daisy glanced up to find Barb giving her the same, narrow-eyed glare she was legendary for sporting in courtroom battles. It was the same one that nine times out of ten preceded witnesses spilling their guts. "You can quit with the look, Barb. I've already told you everything."

Her friend's dubious expression said she wasn't buying Daisy's explanation. "Define *everything*…."

KOLT SMITH, FRESH OFF THE BUS from a week spent at Camp Redwood, couldn't wait to get to his room.

Camp was fun and all, but he'd missed his toys. Some of the guys in his cabin had said they were too old for toys and spent most of their summer chasing girls, but Kolt thought girls were gross—except for his mom. Oh—and Aunt Barb who always gave great birthday and Christmas presents.

"Slow down!" his mother yelled when he raced off the elevator toward their door.

"Can't, Mom! I've gotta pee!"

She not only laughed, but ran alongside him. Very weird when she was usually so serious. Lots of times at night, when she didn't know he was awake, he'd even heard her crying.

"Beat you," she said, tagging the door.

"Yeah, but you cheated by shoving me out of the way."

"I'm a lady," she teased, "and I never shove."

"Whatever." Legs crossed, he hopped. "Just hurry and put in your key."

"I told you to go at Pier Point." Holding open the door, she flipped on the lights.

"Whoa." Their usually cool loft was wrecked. "Did we get robbed?"

"No." She ruffled his hair, usually a sign she was thinking of him as a little kid instead of an almost grown-up. "But as soon as you get out of the bathroom, I do have a surprise for you."

"Is it good?" he asked on his way down the hall crowded with skyscraper piles of boxes.

"I think so. I hope you will, too."

Kolt peed quickly. He was supposed to wash his

hands, but since he wanted to know why there were so many boxes, he just brushed his hands on the fancy towels.

"Okay, what?" he asked, back in the living room.

His mom sucked in a lot of air and then blew it all out. "Well…while you were busy at camp, I was busy, too. Remember when you were little, and I bought you that giant stuffed buffalo and a tepee to play in? And we talked about Oklahoma and how it's an important state?"

"Yeah?" Why did she look as if she was gonna cry? Man, he hated it when she did that. It made his insides feel all twisty.

"There's a reason Oklahoma means more to us than the other states." She wiped her hands on her jeans.

"I know my dad's from there, and those people from the pictures you showed me, but I don't even really know where Oklahoma is."

"That's about to change." She put on a really spooky, big smile. "Honey, I know this is going to be hard for you, but we're moving to Oklahoma, and—"

"What?" Kolt jumped up from the sofa, pitching one of his mom's fancy pillows halfway across the room. "That's stupid! My friend James moved to Chicago and I've never seen him again."

"Honey, calm down and let me explain."

"I don't wanna hear anything. This is because of my stupid dad who I don't even know, isn't it? You're ruining my life! I hate you!" Kolt didn't really hate her, but on the way to his room, he couldn't think of anything better to say. Moving was stupid and so was his mom.

He slammed his door.

She opened it and parked herself on his bed. "Sweetie, there are things I haven't told you that I should've. When I was your age, I had a rough time."

"Why?"

She took a stuffed pig from his toy bucket and played with its ear. "Some day, when you're older, I'll tell you. But for now, I need you to know that when I mentioned all of our relatives lived too far away for us to see, well…"

While she took more really deep breaths, Kolt asked, "You want us to live with them, right? Are we poor or is this supposed to teach me something?"

Standing, she pitched the pig back in his home. "We're not poor and yes, being around people who love you will no doubt prove very educational."

Hating his mom so much he didn't even want to see her, he asked, "How can they love me when they don't even know me?"

"Sometimes…" Her hug smooshed his forehead into her boobs. Why wouldn't she stop and just leave him alone? "When people are family, they love you unconditionally. That's how it's going to be for you. In our new house, you'll have your grandmother and uncles and aunts and there'll be cousins for you to play with."

His friend Lincoln had cousins and they were cool. Every Christmas they stayed with him for like two whole weeks. "Boy or girl cousins?"

"Girls, but—"

"I hate girls!" Just wanting to be by himself, Kolt

ran to the living room, unhooking the safety bar on the
sliding glass door that led to the balcony.

Planted in big pots were little trees.

Kolt hid behind his favorite, not caring that he was
probably sitting in pigeon poop.

He'd been so excited to come home from camp, but
now he wished he could have just stayed there. At least
then he wouldn't have had to move. And he wouldn't
have to see his stupid mom who was making him move.
Or his stupid dad who was the stupid reason his stupid
mom was making them move.

"DAISY. YOU'RE AH, the last person I expected to hear
from." Luke was standing outside a gas station, filling
his truck, on the return leg of a job he'd done in Montana. He hadn't heard from Daisy since their airport
goodbye. Truthfully, she and Kolt had been on his mind
ever since. "Still moving to my neck of the woods?"

"Planning on it, but the transition is going rougher
than I'd like."

"Anything I can do to help?" He topped off his tank,
then fitted the pump nozzle back on its stand. The heat
was intense, shimmering above the blacktop.

"I wish. I'm having a tough time with Kolt. He doesn't
want me to go, and I've tried explaining this is for the
best, but he just doesn't understand." Sighing, she added,
"Sorry to trouble you with this, but I figure since we're
now in this parenting thing together… Well, I'm not
sure why I called. Guess I wanted to hear someone tell
me I'm doing the right thing."

Leaning against his truck, Luke crossed his legs at

the ankles. Stomach knotted, he searched for words appropriate for polite company. "As much as I look forward to my son living closer, you called the wrong person. Truth is, I'm scared for the little guy. You're being too hasty. Not that I know any right or wrong way to handle a kid of his age, but something about this doesn't feel right. You need to slow down."

"Of all people, I thought you would understand. I thought you would want him—us—back in Weed Gulch. Sorry I called."

Out on the highway a trio of eighteen-wheelers rushed by. The exhaust stung Luke's nose. "Don't be like that. You asked my opinion and I gave it."

"No, Luke, what I asked for was compassion and you gave me criticism."

"It's crap like this that keeps me single." Groaning, he shook his head.

Her sharp laugh bit his ear. "Now not only am I ridiculous for wanting to spend time with my family, but I'm putting moves on you?"

"You know damn well that's not what I meant."

"Whatever. I've got to go."

"Daisy, wait—" She'd already hung up.

Luke kicked his tire. The woman was maddening. He hadn't seen her in a decade, yet a few hours spent together and already she was back under his skin. Or, hell, maybe she'd never left.

"WHY ARE YOU CRYING, MOM? Especially since moving was what you wanted to do?"

Two weeks after having decided to move, on the verge

of introducing her son to everyone she held dear, Daisy swiped at tears she'd hoped ten-year-old Kolt hadn't noticed. Forcing a smile, she ruffled his baby-fine dark hair. "Just allergies, sweetie."

"Uh-huh." Usually, she was proud of her smarty-pants son, but this was one time when she wished he wasn't quite so observant.

"Whoa." Though moments earlier his crossed arms had read angry and defensive, he now leaned forward with his hands on the dash. On the maple-lined approach to Buckhorn Ranch's main house, he asked, "Is this like a cowboy mansion?"

The rambling two-story home was large enough for a family of twenty. Until she found a place of her own, no one would even notice she and her son were there.

"Sort of," she answered, pulse racing to an uncomfortable degree. Back in San Francisco, handing over the loft keys to the hip, young artist friend of a friend named Gunter, she'd been positive this wasn't just the right decision, but the only one. Not even her disastrous call to Luke had brought her down. She'd chosen to drive to Oklahoma with Kolt to give him time to transition—not just to the idea of moving, but to the change of climate and scenery.

Stuck in neverending traffic on a six-lane Denver highway, she'd been passed by a father and son and something about the pairing consumed her with chills. What if Luke had a change of heart, deciding he had no interest in becoming an instant father? How would she explain the rejection to her son?

Oklahoma summer sun came as quite a shock to her

body used to San Francisco fog. Though the car's air-conditioning was on high, it had a hard time competing with the sweltering rays.

"Whoever lives here must be *really* rich. Is this where my cousins live?" Kolt angled sideways on his seat to get a better look. "Cool! Look at all the cows! And horses—lots of them! Is that an emu?"

Kolt's excitement shattered Daisy's heart all the more.

She was a horrible mother. The worst. Had she been less of a coward when she'd carried him, he'd have spent every summer and school break on the land where she'd grown up and, in what seemed like another lifetime ago, fallen in love with his father.

"This place is awesome! How come we've never been here on vacation?"

Parking her Mercedes in the circular drive, she turned off the engine and prayed for courage to leave the car.

"Come on!" Kolt prodded, tugging her hand. "There're chickens, too."

From the home's front door barreled the twins, Betsy and Bonnie. Behind them came Dallas and Josie. Next, came Daisy's mom, Georgina, tall and strong, wearing her long white hair in its usual braid—this time neat as a pin.

"Aunt Daisy!" the twins cried in unison, bouncing around her when her quivering legs surprised her by actually allowing her to exit the car. "We missed you!"

"I missed you, too," she said, gathering them for a hug. It warmed her that they even remembered her name.

Kolt rounded the trunk, shyly standing alongside her, taking her hand.

"Who are you?" Bonnie asked.

"Who are *you?*" Kolt retorted.

"Betsy, Bonnie…" Forcing a breath, Daisy looked to her mother and brother. "This is my son, Kolt." His age combined with Luke Montgomery's unmistakable robin's-egg-blue eyes reminded all the adults assembled of everything they needed to know regarding the boy's parentage. "Honey," she said to her pride and joy, cupping Kolt's shoulders, "this is your grandmother and cousins and aunt and uncle."

Eyebrows furrowed, Kolt looked up at her. "Oklahoma wasn't as far as I thought. If they're our family, how come we're just now seeing them?"

Daisy's mother winced as if she'd been slapped.

"Girls," Josie said to the twins, "could you please show Kolt your fort?"

"Boys aren't allowed," Bonnie informed her with a glare in Kolt's direction.

"They are now," Dallas said with a light swat to the girl's behind.

"Come on," Betsy said, sweetly taking her cousin's hand. "We have lots of way-cool stuff."

Kolt looked to Daisy for reassurance—especially about the hand-holding.

"Go on," she nudged, despite the dread knotting her stomach. Hellish Oklahoma sun bearing down on her, she forced a cheery, "Have fun!"

"Okay…" After a last baleful glance, Kolt took off

with Betsy in the direction of the wooded knoll where Daisy had once played with her brothers.

"He's a good-looking boy." Dallas's tone lacked the slightest trace of civility. "Might've been nice meeting him while he was still in diapers."

Their mother silently wept with her hands over her face.

While rubbing Georgina's back, Josie shot her husband a glare.

"What?" Dallas barked at her. "Is it wrong of me to still be pissed? I can see her being freaked out by her pregnancy, but for ten years? We an embarrassment now that you're a big-city lawyer? I thought I was over it, but now..." He shook his head. "I don't even know you. No polite words even describe the damage you've done, not just to everyone you've ever known, but your own damned son."

"Hon..." Hand on his forearm, Josie urged, "that's enough. Daisy had her reasons."

"*Reasons?* Like there could ever be a logical excuse for pulling something like this?" After a sarcastic snort, he wrenched free of his wife to storm off toward the barn.

"Mom, I—" How many times had Daisy rehearsed this moment in her mind? Literally thousands. Yet words wouldn't come. Every horrible thing her big brother had said of her was right. Living with the guilt had become debilitating, interfering with everything from her work to raising Kolt. Each time she looked at her son, she saw his father's eyes, her own father's features.

"He's so handsome—Kolt. Seeing him... It reminds

me how much we've missed. How much your actions stole from us. I'm sorry. I thought I was prepared for this—meeting my grandson, but as happy as I am, I'm also beyond disappointed in you. More like disgusted. You and I used to be so close. We told each other everything. Did you think I wouldn't understand? Not do everything within my power to help? You were only having a baby. Around Weed Gulch, it happens all the time."

Daisy wasn't sure how to respond. While her conscience nudged her to reveal the truth finally, fear kept her lips pressed tight. Daisy had known full well her mother would've moved heaven and earth to help her during her pregnancy. But she would have encouraged her to marry Luke, and that would mean staying on the ranch. She loved this place, but Henry was there and she couldn't have faced carrying a child and seeing him every day. Plus, what if she'd had a girl? What if he'd tried starting the sick cycle all over again?

Chapter Five

Luke Montgomery killed the Weed Eater's motor, lowering his hat brim, shielding the worst of the sun from his eyes. From his vantage atop the hill overlooking his family land, he could see a rising dust cloud, alerting him company was coming. At this distance, he didn't recognize the car, but in his line of work, that wasn't all that unusual.

Knowing he had a full five minutes before the vehicle reached his place, Luke continued with his chore. With his Montana trip it'd been weeks since he'd done any work around the cabin, and truthfully, it felt good having a few days to himself.

As the vehicle drew nearer, he toyed with the notion of at least putting on a shirt, but in the end figured it was too damned hot to bother. At only nine in the morning, he'd hoped the predicted hundred-degree temperatures would hold off long enough to at least let him finish taming the yard. Ha.

By the time the dust-covered Mercedes stopped on his drive, Luke had finished the areas around the cabin's front porch and most of the sides. He shut off the two-cycle engine. No way was he tackling the backyard until early evening.

A woman exited the car. No, not just any woman—the one who'd forever changed his life's course. In the time since he and Daisy had been reacquainted, he'd never seen her look like this.

In the old days, he'd have called out something flirty, like declaring her a cool drink of water. Now, he merely wondered why she'd bothered coming by without his son.

"Where's Kolt?"

"Cash took him and the girls to the swimming hole." Emerging like a cautious bloom from her air-conditioned ride, she was the antithesis of his simple, country way of life. Her big-city garb consisted of a silky white blouse and pearls paired with a pencil-thin dark skirt and heels tall enough to bring the top of her head even with his whisker-stubbled jaw.

Acting on pure instinct, he leaned the Weed Eater against the nearest oak, and then closed the distance between them. He might not like her, but he was incapable of staying away. "When are you planning on letting me see him? Dallas called yesterday, not an hour after you got here. Might've been nice had you at least invited me to share in his first Weed Gulch dinner."

"I came over to clear the air between us, apologize for the umpteenth time, but when it comes to you, I can't do a damned thing right."

"True. But being a gentleman, I won't stop you from tryin'." Long dark hair his fingertips itched to touch had been imprisoned in a fancy knot. Back when she'd been his, he'd liked her to wear it down. "Kolt settling in okay?"

"Yes. Having a ball with his cousins and uncles. He's never been on a ranch before, so for him, this is the equivalent of country Disney world."

"Good." Luke was happy for his son, but again peeved that Daisy had left him out of the family welcome. He'd had every right to be in attendance. No doubt that's why she was here, trying to smooth things over.

Clearing her throat, she finally got around to closing her car door, and then gestured to the cabin's front entry. "Mind if we get out of this heat? There's something I'd like to, ah, run by you."

"Sure. Come on in." He held out his hand to help her up the few steps in those treacherous heels of hers, but she politely sidestepped him to tackle the job on her own. Classic Daisy.

He opened the door for her, thankful for the rush of cool air. "Best thing I ever did was outfit this old place with central heat and air."

"No kidding." She fanned herself. "Feels amazing. I'd forgotten how intense Oklahoma summers can be."

"Yeah, well…" Covered in sweat and dust and grass clippings, he parked himself on the fieldstone hearth.

She chose his favorite armchair.

He said, "You had something to run by me?"

"I do." The oddest look clouded her features. Sadness mixed with fear on top of…shame? She looked around. "You've worked miracles on this old place. When we were kids, it was practically abandoned. You and Dallas and Wyatt used to be so mean to Cash and me if we even came near *your* cabin. Made us wonder what kind of trouble was going on up here."

He chuckled. "We did nearly burn the place down trying to build a still." His mind's eye saw Daisy the way she used to be. A nosy kid always underfoot. She'd been in the same grade as him in school, but because he was friends with her older brothers, Daisy had seemed younger. Then she'd grown. Gangly legs turned long and lean and sun-kissed. Tomboy-short hair morphed into luxurious waves that he'd loved running his fingers through. Daisy's leaving had been a devastating blow. One he'd tried to solve by replacing her.

Tried being the key word.

"How could I forget?" she said with a faint smile. "Dallas mixed that firewater with my morning orange juice and somehow I was the one grounded for a week."

They smiled at one another for a moment. Then Luke shook his head and asked, "So…how's the move in going? I'm surprised you have time to reminisce with me over moonshine and a brother whom I can't ever remember you being all that fond of."

"You know I love Dallas."

"Of course, you do. But do you *like* him?"

She looked away.

"He's a great guy, Daisy. Solid through and through. Now that you're back, you should try getting to know him the way a sister should."

"I know," she snapped.

"Why so defensive? It was just a suggestion."

Standing, she headed for the door.

"Leaving? So soon?"

"I should never even have come." Hand on the door latch, she had trouble getting it open.

"It sticks." Behind her, brushing against her, he ever so deliberately placed his hand over hers, jimmying the hardware. Electricity sizzled between them, so hot it wasn't a far stretch to fairly smell the nitrogen from a summer storm. It'd always been like that. Plenty of chemistry, but no communication. For an indulgent moment, Luke ignored the task at hand to focus on the sweet curve of Daisy's back. The way she still fitted perfectly against him as if she'd been made solely for his pleasure.

"I have to go," she said.

"Unpacking to do?"

She shook her head.

"Then what?" he asked in a voice hoarse with confusion as to why he was suddenly consumed with the elegant sweep of her neck.

"I'm not sure. I'm just busy. *Very* busy." Was it wrong of him to have noticed she still hadn't budged so much as an inch? Just as he'd always had a knack for understanding nature, he used to wield that same talent with her. Leaning against him, she sighed and confessed in a barely audible whisper, "Y-you have to know leaving you wasn't easy. Point of fact, it was the hardest thing I've ever done."

"Then why'd you go?"

"I had no choice."

"Liar." With everything in him Luke wanted to spin her around and kiss her as if the past ten years didn't hang between them like impenetrable curtains. But they did. Daisy Buckhorn never did anything without a reason, starting with parking her fancy car in his drive.

"I have to go." She gave the latch a hard jiggle, and this time succeeded in opening the door. Once outside, she hightailed it to her car. "I'll give you a call about visiting Kolt."

As abruptly as she'd reappeared in Luke's life, she'd just as efficiently exited. Question was—why?

"I HATE THIS CAMP and this hick town," Kolt announced that afternoon upon entering the car. "When can we go home?"

"This is our home," Daisy said with forced cheer that was getting harder and harder to summon. Navigating Weed Gulch Community Center's traffic was no easy feat. At Kolt's previous camps, along with his friends, he'd been picked up and delivered.

Like a pizza.

Another reason for the move—beyond the obvious of having Kolt finally get to know his father and her family—was so Daisy could spend more time with him, as well. The faster her career had grown, the more she'd relied on paying strangers to raise her son.

"I was IM-ing Warren last night, and he and Phillip are going to spend the rest of the summer at Warren's beach house. Why can't I go with them?"

"Because you're going to have a great time here.... Just as soon as I figure out how to get around this busted piece of crap blocking our way." When honking her horn did nothing but make the driver in front of her slow all the more, Daisy sighed. Why had she moved back to this town? Oh, yeah, to reconnect with the family who now barely spoke to her.

"But going to the beach would be way more fun than the crap I'm doing here."

"Did you learn that word today?" She finally had room to pass and gunned the powerful engine.

"No. But since you just said it, why can't I?"

"Because I said so." Traffic around the feed store slowed to a crawl. Were they giving away free samples of cattle chow?

"That's not a good reason. Last time I said that, you told me a judge would never allow that in court."

"Sweetie," she said through gritted teeth, "just this once, please do as I say, and not as I do."

"Okay," he agreed, "but since you really didn't even do anything, then—"

The driver of a forest-green Jeep waiting to make a left out of the feed store's lot honked at her, casually waving his hand out his window.

"Mom, isn't that Luke?"

Unfortunately, yes.

She'd gone to his cabin with the intention of telling him everything—about why she'd left, about Henry. How terrified she'd been of the man following through with the threats to hurt her family. Instead, she'd been so flustered by petty bickering and plain old sexual tension she hadn't been able to think, let alone bare her soul.

"AVOIDING ME?" Thirty minutes later, when Daisy opened the front door of Buckhorn Ranch's main house,

Luke removed his hat and rummaged his hands through his hair.

"O-of course not," she said, stepping out onto the covered front porch and shutting the door. "Why would you think that?"

"Back in town I waved. I saw you had Kolt with you and thought we might grab a malt or something, but you sped off like a spring twister was dogging your heels."

"Was that you?" She flashed him her brightest smile. "Truthfully, I was so fed up with traffic, I hardly even noticed." Laughing, she added, "I grabbed a few things from the store for Mom, picked up Kolt from the day camp I enrolled him in and then hightailed it back here for peace and quiet."

"Why'd you do that? Stick him in a stupid camp when I'd like nothing better than to spend time with him?"

"Good question. One I wish I had an answer for."

Luke had always appreciated honesty, but in this case he might've preferred that Daisy lie. "What's that mean?"

"I don't even know." Taking him by his arm, she dragged him toward the swing. Honeysuckle growing up the side of the house damn near choked him with cloying sweetness. With not a breath of wind, it had to be pushing a hundred if not more. The house's central air-conditioning unit kicked on with a low hum. "He's doing great here at home, but I want him to meet boys his own age. He hasn't mentioned you, and I'm not sure what that means."

"Ouch." His denim-covered thigh brushed hers. She

wore shorts. His memory told him the inside of her creamy thighs felt like satin to his work-roughened palms. Needing to stay focused on the topic at hand, he asked, "How 'bout taking a stab at deciphering his behavior? I mean, I'm all for giving him time to adjust, but you have to know—he has to know—I fully intend on being a big part of his life."

"I understand." It didn't escape him that though she could've scooted a good six inches to the swing's opposite end, she didn't. "I'll talk with him tonight."

"Good. Because it's not just me wanting to meet him, but my family. Trust me, my mom's not going to be held off much longer."

"I know." She stared off to the south pasture where two calves bucked and played in the blazing sun. "We'll plan something soon. I just feel buried. I need to start a practice. Get a place of our own. These things take time. And I suppose if Kolt never really adjusts, there's always the possibility of us returning to San Francisco."

"You didn't burn bridges?" *Like you did with me?*

He was attracted to her like moth to flame, but wary.

His heart knew better than to get too close. Every once in a while in his horse-whispering profession, he came across a mount that refused to be tamed. Daisy had always been a lot like that. Just when he'd thought he had her all figured out, she'd run off. Worse yet, as wild horses were prone to do, she'd emotionally bit him, kicked him, stomped him to the ground. Mustangs were a dangerous breed. He wasn't stupid. He knew it was the danger in them, the thrill of the conquest that kept him coming back. But in Daisy's case, he'd long since learned to appreciate her from afar.

What he didn't want was to be in the same situation with his son. They both deserved better. Daisy may have had her issues, but Kolt didn't deserve to inherit them, and Luke wasn't about to suffer through them by default.

"No, no burned bridges," she said with a dreamy, faraway look, snapping his attention back to the present. "Too much at stake for that."

"Like what?" Surely there wasn't that much involved in hanging out her legal shingle in a two-bit town like Weed Gulch?

"You wouldn't understand."

"Try me."

She sighed. "I don't mean to be rude, but—" She stood, then covered her face with her hands. "I can't do this. Not now. Could you please go?"

"Daisy..." Also on his feet, Luke wanted to pull her into his arms for a comforting hug but he held back. As it was, the exchange had brought on an uneasy sense of déjà vu. The woman had destroyed him once, and he sure as hell didn't plan on letting her do it again. After a catchall nod in her direction, he slapped his hat on his head and walked away.

"I'M SORRY," DAISY SAID to the real estate agent with a light shake of her head. "Would you mind repeating that last bit?" Though it'd been twenty-four hours since her run-in with Luke, Daisy hadn't been able to think straight since.

"Fifteen hundred square feet with a reception area, restroom and two private offices. Rent is six hundred per month, plus utilities and a thirty-dollar-per-month interior greenscape fee for common areas. Margot, down at Fun Flowers in Hawthorne, does a beautiful job decorating for all major holidays."

"I'll take it," Daisy said.

"I have four others to show you," the agent noted, fanning herself with a stack of listing files. "One is in the new Villa Italiana shopping center alongside Reasor's grocery. Très chic."

"Thank you, but I've always liked this building." It was the sole survivor of the 1928 tornado that'd taken out the rest of downtown. The three-story, square brick building had long since been remodeled to combine historic flavor with modern convenience. That said, original pressed-tin ceilings and all of the hand-carved woodwork in the world wouldn't have been charming enough to make Daisy occupy the offices if they hadn't also featured nice cold central air.

"Great," the agent said. "I'll draw up papers and have you in by this afternoon."

"Perfect."

Three hours later, Daisy directed the moving company that had held the contents of her San Francisco loft to cram most of the boxes into the suite's spare office for her to sort through later. She'd decided to store everything in her office until she found a house for herself and Kolt.

By the time Daisy had to pick up Kolt from day camp, the once serene suite had become a maze of boxes and stacked furniture. Leaving the movers on their own, she headed over to the community center, glad for the break.

"What happened to you?" was the first thing from her son's mouth as he climbed into the car.

A glance in the rearview mirror showed that Daisy didn't look much better than her new office. Dust smudged her right cheek and chin and her ponytail resembled an old straw broom. Laughing, she said, "I found an office."

"You look like it attacked you."

"Love you, too," she said with a poke to his belly. "How was camp? Any better?"

"I guess." He slid on his seat belt. "We had to sit in a circle and tell people where we live. I told them San Francisco, but the camp lady said I had to be from here. Well, when I told the other kids I live at Buckhorn Ranch, you should've seen their eyes. It was like I was famous, or something. They were all, like, asking what it was like and five kids want Uncle Cash's autograph."

"Around here," she said, trying not to lose it while navigating between SUVs and minivans, "the Buckhorn name carries a lot of meaning. Your grandfather not only found oil, but raised more cattle than anyone else in town. When I was your age, he and Grandma hosted huge summer picnics, inviting the whole town."

"Why doesn't she do that anymore?"

"Times are different, I guess. Life around here used to be much simpler. There weren't so many other distractions like video games and home theaters. We used to do a lot more activities together."

"Sounds fun." From his T-shirt pocket, he took a green-apple piece of Laffy Taffy. "Want a bite?"

She leaned over and nibbled off a candy sampling.

"How come our last name is Smith, but everyone else in our family is named Buckhorn?"

Daisy's stomach roiled. One more thing to add to her growing to-do list—changing both of their names. Or would Luke want Kolt to take his surname?

"And how come everyone's always calling you Daisy, when your real name's Julie?"

"It's complicated."

"I'm sick of you always saying that." Arms crossed, lips pressed into what was rapidly becoming his customary frown, he asked, "Can we get ice cream?"

"Maybe once we're done with the movers." After parking in her assigned spot behind her new building, Daisy ushered Kolt up a short flight of stairs leading to the rear entrance. After a brief elevator ride, they'd reached her office where the three-man crew folded packing blankets.

"Ma'am," the man in charge said to Daisy, "we're about finished up if you'd like to inspect the furniture and last few boxes for damage."

"Um, sure," Daisy said as Kolt began playing his PSP in the reception area. The task took longer than expected and by the time she'd finished, Kolt had fallen asleep. His hair had grown out and she swept a lock free from his eyes.

Though Daisy knew she'd had no choice but to finalize her business with the movers, this was the sort of thing that'd happened too often in her old life. Now, she hoped to be able to put Kolt first. In the same regard, whether Kolt wanted to or not, he had to spend time with his father.

Daisy wanted that, but she also wanted Luke to know the truth about why she'd left town. With Henry temporarily at the Oklahoma City stockyards, she hadn't been worried about a chance encounter with him, but she was very much concerned with Luke's opinion of her. For Kolt's sake, she wanted the three of them to feel as much like a family as possible. Obviously, that wouldn't happen until Luke not only understood her reasons for keeping Kolt from him, but forgave her.

Chapter Six

"What a nice surprise." Luke opened his door to find Daisy and Kolt on his porch. "I've missed you," he said to his son. As for Daisy, the jury was still out on what he felt for her. Most days, his opinion changed hourly.

"Yeah," Kolt said, shifting his weight from one leg to the other, refusing to make eye contact. One hand was shoved in the pocket of cargo shorts, the other held a black PSP.

"I've given up working on my new office and just picked up Kolt from camp. Anyway," Daisy said with forced brightness, "I thought we'd stop by."

"I'm glad." He flattened himself to the door while both she and his son brushed by. Even the other afternoon when she'd worn shorts, they'd been dressy. Today, in dirt-smudged jeans and an equally filthy T-shirt with her hair a fingered-through mess, she looked as hot as usual, but more approachable. "Can I get you anything to eat or drink?"

"No, thanks." Kolt didn't bother looking up to respond.

Though Luke wasn't happy to see he had his work

cut out for him in getting to know his son, he was some-what encouraged by the fact that Daisy had been telling the truth about Kolt's skittish behavior, rather than just thinking his son had been avoiding him.

Glancing at the half-loaded bins on the kitchen pass-through bar, Daisy asked, "Going somewhere?"

"A job in south Texas. Mare got caught in a lightning storm. Been spooked ever since." He added a can of spaghetti to the nearest bin. "I've got an old Airstream trailer I usually stock and take with me to stay in. More comfortable than a motel and keeps me on the horse's property."

Nodding, she rummaged through the rest of his canned goods. "You should eat better."

He frowned. "I get by okay."

Kolt perched on the sofa arm to play his game.

"Yeah, but baked beans and Vienna sausages? Your arteries are going to solidify."

"Kind of you to care." He nudged her aside before placing the lid on top of the tub, snapping it tight.

"I do care. We've been friends a long time."

"Have we?" He hefted the box off the counter and added it to the pile he had by the back door. "Because, silly me, not hearing from you for a decade had me wondering."

"He's right, Mom." Kolt looked up, for an instant meeting Luke's gaze before darting his attention back to his game. "You could've at least called."

Sitting on one of the counter stools, ignoring their son, she set her keys jingling against the tile. "I've been busy. And anyway, Luke, you were the one who went and got married months after I left."

On that blast from the past, he had to chuckle. "Really? Ten years later *you're* holding a grudge? How'd you even find out?"

Glancing away, she sighed. "Clearly, we shouldn't have come."

"Why? Because I'm so impossible to deal with? I'm not as *civilized* as you?"

"Stop." Heels of her hands to her forehead, she asked, "Can we just start over? The last thing I wanted was for us to fight."

"Me, neither," Kolt mumbled.

"Who's fighting?" Luke asked, taking an ice cream sandwich from the freezer. Daisy used to love them. His mom would buy them and whenever Daisy came over to watch movies or play video games, his dad had teased her about having to guard them from her. "Want one?" he asked his son.

"Sure," Kolt said with a shrug.

After handing one to his boy, Luke offered a treat to Daisy.

"Why would I want ice cream at a time like this? We're right in the middle of—"

"A time like what?" Luke licked the melting parts around the chocolate edges. "We having a crisis?"

After making a sexy little growling noise, she hopped up from her stool, not only helping herself to his freezer, but granting him a tempting backside view. "I've blocked what a nightmare it is dealing with you."

"Whoa," he said while she unwrapped her snack.

"Lest you've forgotten, you're the one who showed up on my doorstep. Right after that, you attacked my diet, then raided my freezer. From where I'm standing, I'm not the one with the problem." Especially since he wasn't counting his sudden and ridiculous fascination with the speck of chocolate clinging to her lower lip.

"Never mind." Ice cream sandwich in one hand, she maneuvered her free hand through her purse handle, then grabbed her keys. "Kolt, you ready to go?"

"Geez, Mom." He crammed the last of his ice cream into his mouth. "You need to chill."

Luke grinned. "Kolt, I think the two of us finally found something we can agree on."

BY THE TIME DAISY REACHED the main road, she was a trembling mess. She'd been stupid to even have gone to Luke's. Especially with Kolt. More than anything, she wanted Luke to know what had happened with Henry. Judging by her irrational behavior, she suspected she was more to blame than Kolt for his inability to get to know his father.

"What's wrong with you?" her son asked as they pulled up the ranch's main drive.

"I'm tired," she said.

"Yeah, well, you're acting weird. Like, I thought we went over to Luke's house for us to all, like, sit around and talk and stuff, but then we just left." He licked chocolate from his right pinkie. "I wasn't really wanting to do all that, but Uncle Cash said Luke has a cool horse, so that might've been fun to see."

And as usual, Daisy had botched things up between

Kolt and his father. "I'm sorry. Why didn't you say you wanted to stick around? You could've done something besides play your game."

"What was I supposed to say? You act like I should instantly like all of these people because they're family, but I've never had family besides you, so I'm never sure what to do."

Putting the car in Park, Daisy killed the engine and pulled her son into a hug. "Sweetie, I love you. Please know you can talk to me about anything you're feeling."

For too short a time, he returned her hug, but then quickly squirmed free. "Stop. Uncle Wyatt's here, and I don't want him to see me all hugging and stuff."

Kolt bounded out of the car, and Daisy was on her own to take her purse and the few legal briefs she'd brought home for scintillating late-night reading from the backseat.

"Hey," Wyatt said, crossing the lot to her. "This kid of yours tells me he's never seen an oil well. Mind if we grab the twins and head out to the ridge?"

"Can I, Mom? Please?" For all of Kolt's complaints about how tough it was getting to know family, when it came to his uncles and cousins, he was fitting right in.

"Go on," she said.

"I'll bring him back in one piece," Wyatt promised.

"Never doubted you wouldn't," Daisy truthfully replied.

Inside, instead of finding her mother and a nice, long conversation, as she'd hoped, she found Josie, who conveyed that chef's salad waited for her in the fridge, that

Georgina was at a church meeting, and that, with their newfound freedom, she and Dallas were off to a neighboring town to see the latest action-adventure flick.

Restless, antsy, Daisy figured what better way to work off nervous energy than by returning to her office for more unpacking? Before setting out, she called Wyatt's cell. He and the kids were in his open-air Jeep and judging by the laughing shrieks, no one was in a hurry to get home.

At quarter past seven, traffic in town was nearly nonexistent and her building's lot was empty. After hours, office suites were accessible through the back entrance and had been wired to a separate security system than the bank. Upon entering a simple code, she was in.

Movers had stashed kitchen, dining room, bathroom and bedroom items in the spare office, meaning all Daisy had to contend with were living room and den furniture and boxes.

She'd hoped the work of arranging and sorting and repacking would keep her mind from straying to Luke. Unfortunately the man wouldn't leave her in peace.

Luke hadn't just been her boyfriend, but her world. In retrospect, leaving him, knowing she was carrying his child, had been beyond stupid. It had been selfish.

But why couldn't she just spill the whole truth and get on with her life?

How come every time she locked gazes with Luke's powerful blue stare, her insides turned to mush and memories of better times consumed her? Even an act as seemingly benign as sharing ice cream sandwiches recalled a lazy summer afternoon when they'd lounged on his bed, feeding them to each other.

Luke's mother, Peggy, had been out of town at a church conference and for a change of scenery, his dad had gone along. Her parents had believed she'd spent the weekend with a Tulsa friend.

Home alone, Daisy and Luke had played house. Cooking together, cleaning together, making love and bathing together… Best of all had been waking up together. Being held safe in his strong arms.

That weekend had been but a teasing glimpse into the life they might have shared if it hadn't been for the fear Henry had made a permanent fixture in her. She was pretty sure Kolt had been conceived that long weekend. Just as she was sure that if she'd told Luke of her pregnancy, she would never have left. Daisy had been so afraid of carrying a girl that all she could focus on at that time had been her escape.

Her office door creaked open and in walked the source of her current dilemma. Luke, in all of his handsome glory. "Henry said I might find you here."

"He's back? He knows I leased office space?"

"Yeah. You know Dallas gossips like an old woman. Besides me, Henry's one of his best friends."

Panic swelled in Daisy's chest, making it hard to breathe. She'd long since told herself she wasn't that scared girl anymore. But the mere knowledge that her nightmare was back on the ranch left her pulse racing and her mouth dry.

Sighing, Luke perched on the arm of the sofa he'd last occupied in her loft. Rubbing his whisker-stubbled jaw, he mused, "I honestly don't know what to make of you."

"Did I hire you to psychoanalyze my every move?" Turning her back on him, she returned to her task of unwrapping framed photos, only to stop. Kolt grinned in every shot. Kolt as a chubby baby. His first day of kindergarten. Hamming it up with his friends on his riotous seventh birthday. Stacking the images, she carefully placed them upside down before returning them to the box. The last thing she needed was for Luke to be reminded of how many precious moments he'd missed. "Sorry. I didn't mean to snap."

"That's my point," he said. "Even though we've been apart for years, I like to think I knew you better than just about anyone. But this version of you—flighty, always on edge—makes me worry."

"Thanks," she said with a sad laugh, "but I'm good." *Are you?*

If Daisy didn't tell Luke—her mom, Dallas, everyone—soon, the weight of her secret would eat her alive. She wasn't sleeping. Rarely ate. Her heart constantly raced as if she'd spent hours running in hot sun.

"If you say so…" Glancing at their surroundings, he noted, "The stuff from your loft doesn't exactly match this building's turn-of-the-century ambiance."

"I probably should've sold it before moving out here." She sat on one of a matching pair of designer lounge chairs upholstered in a black-and-white pinto-patterned leather that had reminded her of home. But since she'd been here, could she really say Weed Gulch was where she belonged? She felt in limbo. Never more so than when she and Luke shared the same air.

"What had you in such an all-fired hurry to leave this afternoon?" The faded denim shirt he wore rolled up at the sleeves worked magic with his blue eyes. The same color looked equally as impressive on his son. Luke had given her the perfect opening to tell him about Henry, so why was her tongue refusing to work?

"I, um, guess I was preoccupied with getting back here to work."

"Which has me wondering…" He rose and crossed the room to sit on the box of books alongside her. "Why so many treks to my house, acting as if there's something pressing on your mind, yet you never say a damned meaningful thing."

"Please, stop," she begged, sliding her hands into the hair at her temples. "It's complicated—my reasoning."

Leaning in, close enough for her to have sworn she caught a hint of sweet ice cream still on his breath, he said, "I'm a big boy. You'd be surprised how much I might understand." His nearness transported her back to a time before Kolt. Before fear had gotten in the way of love. Back to when she'd wanted nothing more from life than to spend her every waking moment in Luke's arms. To when she'd believed a life with him protecting her would forever keep her from harm.

"You can admit it," he said, still too close for her mind to function properly.

"Wh-what?"

"You're flustered about being close to me." Cupping her cheeks, he kissed her.

Yes! the teen girl in her cried.

No! warned the world-weary professional she'd become.

"I am, too—about being around you, but see? We
kissed and nothing happened. No sparks. Not a single
firework or marching band. So now that we have that
established, we can get down to the business of setting
up a formal visitation schedule for Kolt."

"Whoa. Time out." She pushed him from her in a
frantic search for air. Standing, hands on her hips, she
paced. How dare he toy with her this way. As if he knew
how flustered he made her and wanted her to squirm.
"What the hell was that?"

"I told you. Just clearing the air."

"Hello, there."

Kolt looked out the window of the awesome fort
that used to belong to his uncles to see Henry. Uncle
Dallas had introduced them and told Kolt what a cool
guy he was. Adjusting his pirate eye patch, Kolt said,
"Hi, Henry!"

"Permission to climb aboard, Cap'n?"

Kolt laughed. "Yeah! I didn't know you knew how
to play pirates."

"I play all kinds of fun games," Henry said, climbing
the fort's ladder. Once he'd made it to the top, he sat on
a wooden crate, and then pulled a Snickers bar out from
under his cowboy hat. "Like candy?"

"You bet. Thanks!" While Kolt chewed, Henry took
a pocket knife and a small block of wood from his back
pocket.

"Uncle Cash said he's gonna get me a knife, but I have to ask my mom first."

The old guy nodded. "Always a good thing to ask your mom. When she was little, we used to play all the time. Now that you're here, I'm sure she'd want me to be great friends with you."

"That's cool." Kolt handed Henry his favorite sword. "Do you want to be the good guy or the bad guy?"

Henry took a long time to answer, but then smiled. "I want to be the good guy, you naughty little pirate. That way I can teach you the proper way to treat a gentleman."

"Argh!" Kolt said in his best pirate voice. "You'll never tame me."

FIVE DAYS LATER AND Daisy still couldn't stop thinking of Luke's kiss. *Clearing the air?* Of what? Sexual tension? Had that indeed been his plan, it hadn't worked— at least not for her.

More than ever, Luke was on her mind, but then so was Henry. So many old, frightening feelings coursed through her. Part of her wanted to work toward earning Luke's forgiveness and possibly forging a family with their son. Another part knew that fairy tale would never happen. Henry wasn't just in her nightmares, but living a couple of hundred yards from her bedroom in his tidy little house.

She had never needed Luke more.

But she also knew if he were one day to forgive her for hiding his son, as soiled as Henry had made her, she didn't deserve to be with a man as good as Luke.

With Luke out of town, Daisy had managed to get her office cleared of clutter and mostly functioning, as well as getting Kolt enrolled for his upcoming year at Weed Gulch Elementary. School documents had never been an issue at his private academy. Here, however, Daisy had received more than a few weighty stares from one old crone in the office whom she was pretty sure had been working as a lunch lady when she had started kindergarten.

Most days Daisy felt as if the whole town were judging her. Condemning her for keeping Kolt from Luke. If they only knew her other dark secret, gossipy tongues would really be wagging. Everyone loved Henry. Would her family and Luke even believe her when she told them what the *kindly* man had done?

"Ready?" Kolt, dressed in brand-spanking-new Western wear purchased for him by his Uncle Cash, practically danced in front of the sofa where Daisy had been flipping through a real-estate magazine.

"Grandma's still on the phone." Patting the empty spot next to her, Daisy asked, "Do your boots feel okay? Nothing ruins a rodeo faster than tight or rubbing boots."

"They're good," he said, demonstrating by wiggling his feet in front of him. "Wonder what my old friends would think?"

"'Bout what?" She smoothed the cowlick in his dark hair. For a moment, she felt as if her breath had been knocked out of her. How had she never before noticed the way Kolt's hair stuck out at the same crazy angles as his father's?

"My cowboy boots and hat and jeans. No one wears stuff like this at home."

"This is your home now, and I promise, if you showed up at the summer rodeo wearing expensive high-tops, shorts and a T-shirt, you'd look like an alien from another planet." She tickled his stomach. His laugh never failed to brighten her spirits.

"Sorry about that," Georgina said, slipping on a silver-and-turquoise bracelet on her way into the living room. "Unavoidable damage control with loose-lipped Frieda Hilliard."

"What's that mean?" Kolt asked.

"None of your nosy beeswax." Kolt's grandmother clamped her hands over his ears while kissing the top of his head. Daisy guessed her mother had been handling more fallout in regard to her. "Did your brother and Josie already leave?"

Daisy nodded. "The girls were bouncing off the walls."

"They are a handful," her mother noted.

"More like crazy," Kolt said, on his feet and practicing quick draws with his plastic revolver. In San Francisco, he'd been all about video games and not much else. Daisy loved how he'd once again started using his imagination since coming to the ranch. "Bonnie tried piercing my ears. Her mom caught her just before I died from that psycho girl stabbing me to death with a safety pin."

"That's awful." His grandmother pulled him into a hug.

"I know," Kolt said, aiming for the stuffed moose

head mounted above the fireplace. "That's why I wanted to ride with you and Mom and Aunt Wren and Robin. That baby bites, but usually I'm fast enough to get away."

"Excellent decision." Daisy grabbed her purse and keys. She'd dressed in a long, full skirt made of light-weight crinkled brown cotton. Her white cotton tank top was ultra-feminine with lacing at the neckline. She wore it over the skirt, topped with a concho belt hanging low at her hips. Her alligator boots were the ones her father had bought her for middle-school graduation. In deference to the inevitable heat, she'd braided her long hair, securing it at the tips with beaded ponytail holders she'd borrowed from the twins. "Cash put Robin's carrier in my car before he left this morning, so as soon as we grab her and Wren, we're good to go."

They drove the short distance to Cash and Wren's house.

"Thanks for the ride," Wren said once they'd reached the main road. "After finally getting a Sunday off, the last thing I felt like doing was driving—even if it is only a short way."

"I understand," Daisy said, adjusting the air conditioning to make it cooler.

"Trying to freeze us out?" her mother complained.

"Sorry." Fanning her face, Daisy said, "It's been a while since I've been in this kind of heat."

From the backseat Kolt asked, "I like the hot weather. Why haven't you brought me here, like, *ever,* Mom?"

Judging by Georgina's pressed thin lips and Wren's sudden fascination with the buttons on Robin's overalls,

Daisy wasn't the only one feeling awkward about the question. Trouble was, as much thought as she'd given the subject, she still didn't have a reasonable, justifiable answer. She couldn't tell her ten-year-old that essentially Mommy had been afraid that if he'd been a girl, the bogeyman might return. Then, by the time she'd discovered she was having a boy, she'd been too ashamed of what she'd let Henry do to return.

"Mom?" Kolt prodded.

Swallowing the knot at the back of her throat and ignoring her mother's silent tears, Daisy said, "For the longest time, I lost the way home, but now that I found it again, we'll be here a nice long while, okay?"

He nodded. "Will there be food at the rodeo? I'm hungry."

"Do you like funnel cake?" Georgina asked with forced cheer.

"I dunno," Kolt said. "Never had it."

That inconceivable fact earned Daisy another glare. The fried, powdered-sugared treat was a rodeo staple.

"Well," her mother said with an extra serving of guilt, "that means we'll have to get you *lots* of them to make up for all the ones you've missed."

EXHAUSTED FROM THE LONG DRIVE, Luke knew better than to get back out on the road for a rodeo. But it was Weed Gulch's annual fundraiser for "Town Beautification," and since his mother was this year's Beautification Chairwoman, she'd have his hide if he didn't at least show up long enough to hand over his money.

Plus, he wanted to be there for his son's first rodeo.

On the downside, the Buckhorn family was always in attendance. Luke hadn't seen Daisy since that kiss. A good thing, since he'd lied like a dog about his not having a reaction. Every time he thought about it, he grew rock hard and grouchy. He hated her for what she'd done. It was high time his body got the message.

This would be the first year since before Duke Buckhorn had died that all four of his children were in attendance with their mother—at least Luke assumed all of them would be there. Aside from Christmas, this event was the pinnacle of the Weed Gulch social season.

Upon reaching the rodeo grounds, Luke parked in what felt like the next county and then zigzagged through screaming kids, rodeo queens and horses. He was just thinking he'd be better off back at his cabin when he caught sight of Daisy, all dolled up in her prettiest country wear.

Kolt stood alongside her, looking as if he'd spent his whole life doing just this thing. Decked out in head-to-toe cowboy, he was handsome as could be. Throat knotted with pride, Luke couldn't wait to show off his son.

As for Kolt's mother, Lord, but she was a beauty. Long legs and an easy smile.

She stood in front of the funnel-cake wagon, waiting her turn in line with Dallas's evil twins, Wren and her baby.

Luke strode up to the group.

"Bonnie," he said, tugging the girl's crooked pigtails, "you buying me a funnel cake?"

"Nooo," she said with a look as offended as if he'd

asked her to give him her pony. "I don't have any money. Aunt Daisy's buying mine and Betsy's."

"Then maybe she'll pay for me?" he said with a wink in Daisy's direction.

Bonnie shrugged.

"How was your week?" he asked Kolt after obligatory greetings to Wren and Bonnie. Was it wrong that part of him damn near feared talking to Daisy? She made him hot and bothered and took his mind from the most important thing on the day's agenda—sharing quality time with Kolt.

Not Kolt's sexy-as-hell mom.

"Thought you couldn't come," Daisy said, hating the way her pulse raced at the mere sight of Luke. She felt the way she had back in high school. Save for the ten years she'd been gone, they'd attended this event together literally every year of their lives.

"Hey," Wren said, waving Robin's chubby hand at Luke.

Luke playfully snatched the baby's hand, pretending to chew.

Robin shrieked with laughter.

Watching him interact with the infant hurt Daisy to her core. Worse yet was the look on her son's face as he saw his father interact more easily with a child who wasn't even his.

"You're looking mighty spiffy," Luke finally said to their son. "I like those cowboy duds."

"Thanks," Kolt said almost pensively. "I didn't know if other kids wore this stuff, but since they do, I like it."

"What events have you seen so far?" Luke asked as they stepped up in line.

"Barrel racing. It's pretty cool. But I'm mostly excited for bull riding. That's what my uncle Cash does."

As a professional bull rider, Cash was ineligible to compete, so he typically hung around back, helping with the chutes.

Wren shook her head. "To my eternal dismay. As if it's not bad enough I have to worry about him smashing his head in wrestling with a bull, he's got so many groupies he could form his own girls' school."

Laughing, Luke said, "And knowing the size of your husband's ego, he loves every minute of it."

Kolt said, "Uncle Cash told me he loves Aunt Wren best, 'cause she kisses like—"

"Whoa there, bud." Cash sauntered up to them, blasting them with his thousand-watt smile. "Don't be spilling all my secrets. You can't let the ladies know how much you like 'em, otherwise that gives 'em leverage to break your heart."

"Oh, stop," Wren said, pummeling her husband with her free hand.

Daisy glanced Luke's way and their gazes locked. For a heady second, hot summer sun melting the sense from her head, everything was back the way it had once been. She was with Luke. Then she remembered he could hardly stand the sight of her. He'd only kissed her to prove all that had once simmered between them was now dead. Only, for her, it should be, but sadly, wasn't.

Moving up in line, Daisy was relieved to have finally

placed their funnel-cake order. Maybe once they'd eaten, Luke would trail off to find his family, and stop distracting her.

"What do you think?" Daisy asked Kolt after he'd taken his first bite of the funnel cake.

All smiles, with his nose and chin white, he said, "This is amazing!"

"Told you so," Betsy sassed. "You're dumb for never eating this stuff."

"Yeah, well, you're dumb and ugly for being a girl."

"Hey!" Daisy warned. "Knock it off."

"It's okay," Bonnie said. "'Cause he's dumb and ugly for being a boy."

While nodding in agreement, Betsy stuck out her white, sugar-coated tongue.

While the rest of the party laughed over the kid antics, for Daisy, the moment had lost its sparkle. Standing not ten feet from her was Henry. Sneaking up behind the girls, he made a mock pounce for them, then tugged their matching ponytails.

"All of you ladies are looking as pretty as the flowers in Georgina's garden." Henry rested his hands on the twins' backs, smiling a clear challenge in Daisy's direction.

Nausea struck clear and hard—stunning in its unexpected blow. She was no longer a strong, confident woman, but a little girl being fondled by a dirty old man.

Lurching to action, Daisy snagged the twins by their arms with enough force to jostle their plates to the packed-dirt ground.

"Get away from him!" Daisy shouted on instinct.

Betsy started to cry.

Bonnie snapped, "Are you crazy? Betsy *loves* funnel cake!"

"I'm sure it was an accident, right, Daisy?" Henry had his filthy hands back on the twins, chuckling as if they were all one, big happy family. "Funny thing about accidents…" With the twins firmly against him, he clamped his hand over Kolt's head. "Never can tell when or where they might strike."

Daisy wanted to hit out in rage, but couldn't. Henry's smile, his voice, paralyzed her with fear. *Please don't touch me.*

"You all right?" Wren asked Daisy. "You've turned white as a sheet."

"Kolt, girls," Daisy said, "it's time to go home."

"What?" Kolt complained. "We just got here."

"I'm not going anywhere with you," Bonnie declared. "You're crazy. Come on, Henry." The girl took the man's hand. "Let's go ride the merry-go-round."

"No!" Daisy managed to choke out.

"Mom, stop!" Kolt said when she tugged him to her, hugging him for all she was worth. "I hate you! You're being weird!"

He wriggled free to run off toward the bull chutes.

"I—I have to go after him," she said on autopilot, determined to save her son.

"Let him go," Luke urged. "Cash is there. He'll watch over him. Right now, I'm concerned about you."

"As am I," Henry said, rubbing his leathery hand

along her bare forearm. "Poor girl. What you need is a nice big hug."

It was too much. The heat. The children being in danger. Henry's awful touch. Daisy's knees buckled as her world faded to black.

Chapter Seven

"I hate her!" Kolt said to a big, black bull with snot running out of his nose. "My mom's ugly and mean and—"

"You'd better watch talking about Mack like that, he's liable to bite your nose."

"Bulls don't bite, Uncle Cash." Kolt looked over to find his uncle looking way cool in his cowboy boots and hat and a huge, shiny belt buckle.

"But your mom does?"

Nose scrunched, Kolt asked, "What?"

His uncle whispered, "She always has been weird. I can't count how many times she's bitten me."

Cracking a smile, Kolt gave his uncle a hug.

"What's that for?"

"I wish you were my dad." Kolt didn't want to cry, but he couldn't help it. The crying just came out.

"Hey, whoa," his uncle soothed, rubbing his back. "There's no crying at rodeos."

"I—I'm sorry," Kolt said.

"I'm teasing. You cry all you want." Scooting over to a bench, Cash hefted Kolt onto his lap. Kolt didn't want to look like a baby, but it sure felt good being loved. Especially now that he didn't have a mom or dad who weren't crazy. "So all joking aside, what happened?"

"Just stuff," Kolt said, thinking back to how nuts his mom had acted and then how his dad hadn't even done anything to stop her. Henry was awesome. Why would she act like that? "I hate both of my parents."

"Since you won't tell me what happened, all I can say for sure is that your mom and dad love you."

Shaking his head, Kolt said, "I know for a fact she doesn't, otherwise every time something fun happens she wouldn't ruin it. I can't even talk to my dad without her flipping out about something. And just now, I was gonna go with Henry and the twins and she freaked out again."

"Hmm." Uncle Cash seemed to think about that. "Maybe she's just having a bad day."

"Yeah, but she has one every day, and that means I never get to see my dad." One of those real fancy rodeo queens passed. Kolt wriggled off Cash's lap to sit beside him. "Do you know him? I mean, like are you friends?"

"Me and Luke?" Cash asked.

Kolt nodded.

"He's a great guy. I've been friends with him my whole life and trust me, if your mom hadn't kept you a secret, he'd have been the best dad any kid ever had— except for me." Uncle Cash winked.

With no girls in sight, Kolt snuggled closer. "Really, I'm just gonna live with you and Wren and Robin now, okay?"

"Much as I'd love having another stud as handsome as myself in the house, that's not going to work. Your mother would have my hide." Cash swatted at a fly. "Not only that, but mark my words, you're going to end up thinking Luke's pretty amazing."

"I don't think so," Kolt said with a firm shake of his head.

"Can you do me a favor and try liking him? Luke's my friend, and I'd hate to have you not like him just because he's not as handsome as me."

Laughing, Kolt said, "You're as crazy as my mom!"

"But darned good-looking, right?"

"WHERE ARE THE KIDS?" Daisy asked, abruptly waking in the shade of an oak, cradled in Luke's capable arms. "Kolt? The twins? They're not with Henry?"

"Whoa," Wren said, checking her pulse. "Let's not have a repeat of whatever just sent you crashing. The twins are with Dallas and Josie, and Kolt's with Cash. Now, drink some water for me and tell me what that spell was about. Has this happened before?"

"Never. I'm fine. But I need to find my son." Daisy sat up, only to have her head swim.

"What's going on with you?" Luke asked. "Why this sudden concern for the kids? This is Weed Gulch. Aside from a few over-eager mini-van moms speeding in a school zone, there's not a lot of crime in this neck of the woods."

If he only knew just what caliber of criminal Henry truly was. A tremble began deep inside, manifesting in her shivering on a dangerously warm day.

"I'm thinking it's time to call an ambulance," Wren said to Luke. Robin cooed on a blanket alongside her.

"No," Daisy snapped. "I'm fine." She shook her head. "Just shaken. Henry—he's not who you think he is."

"What are you talking about?" Wren asked, sitting back on her heels. "Henry's a loveable lug. He's offered to babysit for us a couple of times when we needed someone in a pinch."

Hands cradling her throbbing forehead, Daisy said, "H-Henry's not who you think he is. H-he molested me. O-over and over. E-everyone thinks he's this wonderful man, but he's a monster. I haven't had the courage to tell everyone, but seeing him around the kids... Before he left, he made threats and then just now, when I saw him touching the twins, I—I knew no matter what, the truth had to be told."

"Oh, Daisy..." Wren looked to Robin, placing a protective hand on her tummy.

Daisy felt Luke tense beneath her. Every inch of him hardening as if bracing for a fight. "It all makes sense. You were a walking statistic. The partying. Taking stupid risks. Running away from everyone you loved when you should've run toward us." On his feet, he slammed his right fist into his left palm.

"We have to tell someone," Wren said, expression dazed. "The authorities have to be called."

"D-don't waste your breath." Daisy informed them of the laws that made going after Henry difficult. For a woman as private as Daisy, the stares of passersby should've mortified her, instead, the release of such a long-held secret was liberating.

While racking sobs escaped her, Luke knelt beside her, holding her close. "Let it out... That's it. No one's ever going to hurt you again."

"Wh-when I saw him," she said against Luke's chest, "something in me snapped. On the outside, I've grown so much, but on the inside, I'm still a scared little kid. He told me if I tattled on him, everyone I loved would hate me. Or worse, he'd hurt them. He made threats so many times I ingested his poison and deeply believed it. As much as my brothers love him, I still wonder what if they think I'm lying? After all, it's my word against his. They no doubt view me as their nutty sister who ran off for greener pastures. Meanwhile, there's wise, kind, dependable Henry—does he still carve all those stupid wood toys?"

Lips pressed tight, Luke nodded.

"H-he once told me Christmas was the happiest time of the year for him—not for the usual reasons, but because so many little boys and girls got to sit on Uncle Henry's lap." She shuddered. "Now, can you see why I left? I was eighteen and wild and had been so badly abused my head wasn't on straight. Wh-when I found out I was pregnant, my only thought was running as far as I could. A-and then, the longer I stayed away, the more impossible returning became. I knew I'd disappointed so many people—most of all, you."

"I get it," Luke said, smoothing her hair from her forehead. "Still don't like it, but I understand. Why didn't you tell someone? A teacher, Doc Haven...*me?*"

Back in those days, Luke had loved Daisy with cutting clarity. With her brother as his best friend, Luke had known Daisy his whole life, but the summer before their freshman year in high school, she'd stopped being a pest to become his fascination. Long blond hair, limbs kissed sun-gold, her smile made him aspire to be more than a 4-H kid who spent every spare second with his horse.

"I know," she said barely loud enough for him to hear.

But she didn't—*know.* Henry's actions had had a ripple effect. By causing her to leave, so many more lives had been hurt. Including Luke's. Their son's. Luke had spent years wondering what he'd done wrong. So much lost time and energy and, most of all, hope.

As much as Luke was firmly in Daisy's proverbial court, he also knew that, beloved as Henry was in the Weed Gulch community, folks would take sides. Up to the day she left, Daisy had had a reputation for being the Buckhorn wild child. Now that Luke knew what demons she'd been running from, her constant partying made sense. But would the God-fearing people of Tohwalla County see the accomplished woman Daisy had fought to become? Or would she remain the out-of-control teen they remembered?

"PLEASE, DALLAS, SAY SOMETHING." After pouring out her story in his quiet study, Daisy's pulse raced to an uncomfortable degree. Luke had brought her home while Wren organized the rest of the family, making sure the children were occupied while Daisy delivered her news. "Tell me what's going through your head?"

His sarcastic laugh bordered on dangerous.

Fists clenched, he rose.

"What're you doing?" she asked, also on her feet.

"Getting answers." Already to the study door, he stormed out the house's back exit, his strides too large for her to catch up.

"Dallas, wait!"

He waved off her request. No use in asking him where he was going. Henry's one-bedroom home stood next to the barn. Directly in Dallas's path.

By this time, the rest of the family had taken note of his uncharacteristic behavior. Her mother and brothers, along with Josie and Luke all stood behind her. Wren was with the children in the movie room, where a Disney film blared loud enough to block matters not fit for young ears.

"Henry Pohl," Dallas shouted, banging the heel of his fist against the old man's door.

Though Daisy's rubbery knees threatened to buckle, she, along with the rest of the crowd, trailed after Dallas.

"Get out here!"

"Boss," Henry said with his characteristic slow smile and a tip of his cowboy hat. "To what do I owe this pleasure?"

Dallas delivered a hard right to Henry's jaw.

"What the hell—" Henry adopted a defensive pose.

Daisy was so frightened she forgot to breathe.

Luke sidled up behind her, cupping his hands to her shoulders in silent support.

"Did you mess with my sister?" Dallas asked.

"Absolutely not," Henry said, having the audacity to

look offended. "That what this runaway harlot claimed? How many years have I given to you and yours, Dallas Buckhorn? This kind of insulting accusation is how you repay me?"

"Shut up!" Daisy screamed, childishly placing her hands over her ears. "I can't take any more of your lies. You molested me over and over in this very house. You told me it was our *special* secret, and that if I ever told another soul, I'd be in trouble. Well, you know what, you sick bastard? I'm not afraid or defenseless any more. I let you rob me of the past ten years, but no more. You're never going to do this to another little girl."

"Oh, Daisy…" Her mother crushed her in a hug. "Why didn't you tell us?"

Her story poured out on racking sobs. How Henry had threatened not only her if she'd told, but all of them. In the end, Daisy had felt crazy and had to get away. She'd wanted to come home, but fear and embarrassment and shame all melded into a wall she feared she'd never break through.

To Henry, Dallas said, "You've got fifteen minutes to pack up your crap and get the hell off my land."

"Be reasonable," Henry said. "Clearly, Daisy's not in her right mind."

"Me?" Daisy shrieked. "What you did was unspeakable."

Wrapping her arm around Daisy's shaking shoulders, Georgina said, "Let's get you inside. Dallas, just as soon as that man's gone, call the sheriff."

"Let's not be too hasty," Henry pleaded. "Please. This is my home."

"Dallas," Daisy managed, "from a legal standpoint, there's nothing we can do."

"The hell there isn't," her brother roared. "Ladies, get on in the house and let us men take care of this."

Relieved didn't come close to describing how Daisy felt about her family rallying around her.

"Georgina," Josie said, "I'm going to help Wren with the kids. I'm sure you and Daisy need to talk."

"Thank you," Daisy said to her sister-in-law.

"It's us who should be thanking *you*," Josie said with an awkward hug. "Truthfully, I've heard Henry ask the twins to play at his house, and thought it odd. Now, I know why alarms went off in my head. H-he just seemed so kind. Part of the family, you know?" Hand to her forehead, she sharply exhaled. "Listen to me. I'm babbling. I—I just can't believe this kind of predator has been in our home."

"I know," Daisy said. "I'm sorry I didn't come forward sooner, I just…"

"Shh," Georgina urged. "Now that this ugly business is out in the open, let Dallas take care of it. We need never speak of it again."

As much as Daisy appreciated her mother's kindness, the *ugly business* was an intrinsic part of who she was. Now that those she loved were aware of the reason behind her leaving, she wanted it out of her, and talking about it was the only way to make that happen.

An hour later, exhausted from the showdown with Henry, Daisy lay stretched out on the living-room sofa, resting her head on her mother's lap. "I should still be worried about Henry, but all I can think about is how upset Kolt was at the rodeo. I want him to understand I had good reason, but the last thing I want to do is burden him with my trouble."

"I'm so sorry," Georgina said, softly stroking Daisy's hair. "I feel like I'm at the root of all of this. If only I'd paid closer attention to you, instead of to my garden club and parties, none of this ever would've happened."

There had been a time when Daisy had put the entire blame on her mother's shoulders, but with each passing year, she'd realized how the whole family had been victims of Henry's abuse. "Don't let that guilt settle in. It's counterproductive. I know. For now, I need to focus on Kolt and Luke. I have to help them make up for the time I stole."

"As wonderful a man as Luke is, I suspect Kolt will soon enough grow to love him, and in the process forgive you. But, hon, it's not going to happen overnight."

"I know." Daisy had naively hoped returning to Weed Gulch would create positive changes for her son. He was getting to the age that he needed a man to look up to—not that being with his father wouldn't have been beneficial to him through all stages of his development, just that now that Kolt was soon to be a teen, Daisy wouldn't be his ideal choice for discussing guy stuff. Groaning, she rubbed her throbbing forehead. "I thought telling all of you about Henry would be my hardest task. But now, I'm afraid it wasn't anywhere near as tough as it's going to be ensuring my son grows up happy and well-adjusted."

"YOU CAN TALK TO ME, YOU KNOW."

The night of the rodeo, Kolt didn't even want to look

at his mom, and he sure didn't want to talk to her. He sat on the end of the bed in his new room. The walls were dark green and he missed his old blue room back in the loft.

"I'm sorry if I embarrassed you this afternoon. Henry's not a nice man and all I could think about was getting you away from him."

"He's always been nice to me." What was wrong with his mother? Making up stories about people. Plus, she was always fighting with his dad. Why did he have to be nice to Luke if she wasn't?

She sighed. "I know he may have seemed nice, but on the inside, he's a very bad man. If you ever see him again, run and tell a grown-up as fast as you can."

Kolt rolled his eyes. "I wish Uncle Cash and Aunt Wren could be my mom and dad. They're not crazy. I asked Uncle Cash to take care of me."

"Oh?" She chewed on her fingernails and looked as though she was about to cry. Kolt hated seeing her upset, but lately all she'd done was hurt him. "What did he say about that?"

"He said, no, because I have a mom and dad. But I know if I help Uncle Cash with chores and stuff, he'll want to keep me."

"Get this straight," his mom said in what he now knew was her crazy voice. "You are mine. You will not live with Uncle Cash and you will stop being upset with me for watching out for you the only way I know how. Have I made mistakes? Do I still? Yes. What parent doesn't? But I love you."

"Can I please just go to bed?" Kolt was tired of

hearing her talk. She always said lots of stuff that sounded good, but nothing ever changed.

MONDAY EVENING, through the setting sun's orange glow, Luke saw the dust cloud before the car. Instinct told him exactly who it would be.

He finished watering what remained of his struggling tomato plants, then coiled up the hose. By the time he'd finished, sure enough, Daisy and Kolt had pulled into his drive.

After drying his palms on the thighs of his jeans, Luke moseyed over, not especially in a hurry to see the woman who'd turned his life upside down. He'd had a tough enough time relating to her before learning about what she'd been through with Henry. Now, Luke was even less sure of what to do or say.

She was wearing a T-shirt and pink flip-flops that made her look all of fifteen. Her messy pigtail didn't help. She looked as pretty as she had the spring day he'd asked her to the prom. But that didn't change the fact that as sorry as he felt for what Henry had put her through, she didn't have a free pass for Luke missing the first ten years of his son's life.

When Kolt exited the car, stepping onto his land, Luke wasn't sure what to say. Kolt was handsome. Tall for his age and stick thin. A smattering of freckles dotted his nose and his dark hair had been neatly trimmed.

"When I was your age," Luke said to his boy, hands shoved in his pockets, "I hated getting my hair cut. One day my mom let me cut it myself. Kids at school teased that it looked so bad I must've got caught in barbed wire.

Just looking at your head tells me you're a damned sight smarter than me."

"You cussed," his son scolded.

Chuckling, Luke said, "About time you learned that's what cowboys do. Sometimes there's just no way around it."

"Don't listen to him," Daisy said.

"Do listen to me," Luke insisted with what he hoped came across as a welcoming, friendly smile. "Here's what you need to do. Let's say you're on your horse and see a snake. What're you going to say?"

Nose wrinkled, Kolt shook his head. "I dunno."

"Wrong. How about, damn, that's a big snake."

Wearing a cautious grin, Kolt mimicked, "Damn, that's a big snake."

"Excellent." Luke held out his hand for a high five and was pleasantly surprised when Kolt didn't leave him hanging. "All right, now it's time for—"

"That's enough." Arms crossed, Daisy didn't look amused by the evening's cursing lesson. "Could we please go inside? It's hot."

"Help yourself," Luke said. "Front door's open. If Kolt doesn't mind, we need to feed the horses before we head in for the night."

"Kolt?" she asked, worry lacing her tone. "Is that all right with you?"

"Just go, Mom. I want to talk to my dad."

Luke couldn't help but beam with pride when his boy asked, "Can I brush your horses, too? Uncle Cash taught me how and he says I do a really good job."

"Absolutely," Luke said, ignoring the fact that Daisy

still stood in front of the porch. "And hey, while I've got you here, can you tell me why the farmer's horse went over the mountain?"

"Nope."

"He couldn't go under it."

Though Kolt didn't crack a smile, he couldn't quite hide the light in his eyes.

Luke knew he had a long way to go before his son fully accepted him, but, Lord willing, with enough bad jokes and kid-friendly animal chores, the two of them might work their way into each other's hearts.

As for his child's mother? Good thing Daisy had finally chosen to hide out in the house or Luke just might've put her on manure duty.

Chapter Eight

A week had passed since Daisy's last secret had gotten out. Funny how time had a way of elongating or shortening in direct proportion to one's discomfort level. The past seven days had felt excruciatingly long. Kolt was still giving her the silent treatment, insisting Henry had been his friend. During her brief exchanges with Luke, he wasn't much more communicative.

She'd hoped sharing the whole of her past would bring them closer, but instead, he seemed more distant than ever. Painfully polite, as if mere words might cause her to once again break.

Seated behind what had once been her home desk that she'd placed in the sun-flooded southeast corner of her new office, Daisy tackled a few emails from Barb regarding case research. Her friend had asked her to stay on with the firm at least until Daisy established her own law practice. Barb made no effort to hide her hopes that Daisy would soon tire of small-town life.

Truth be told, though Daisy had never been surrounded by more people who knew her, she had also never felt more lonely or out of place.

Dallas had Josie.

Cash had Wren.

Georgina had club meetings and grandchildren.

Wyatt had his travels and a seemingly neverending stream of buxom blondes.

By comparison, Daisy felt as if she had no one. Sending a personal note grousing about this fact to Barb, Daisy was surprised by her boss's down-home advice to take the bull by the horns and make her son and Luke spend time with her.

Though it'd been years since she'd been on a picnic, Daisy figured that'd be as good a way as any to start the lengthy process of regaining their trust.

"Hey," she said when Luke answered his cell on the second ring.

"What do you need? I'm in the middle of something."

"Sorry. I'll make it quick." She doodled a series of stars on a yellow legal pad. "Are you free tonight? I thought we might build a fire down by the pond and roast hot dogs. Make s'mores." *Talk*.

"Sounds nice," he said, "but I already made tentative plans with Kolt and Cash and Dallas."

"Oh?" Nice of him to include her.

"I was going to call and run it past you, but Dallas said there's some pretty decent catfish in the pond by the Peterson place. We're riding horses over just as soon as Kolt gets home from camp."

Snapping her pencil in half, Daisy managed a count to three in her head before she blew. "While I'm thrilled that you've jumped right into parenting, Luke, you seem to have forgotten the fact that I'm Kolt's primary care-giver. As such, it's customary for you to—"

"Stop right there," Luke said, tone lethally low. "Don't you dare lecture me on how much time I'm allowed with my boy. Within reason, I will see him whenever, and wherever I'd like. As I'm sure you and any right-minded judge would agree, we have lots of lost time to make up for."

Daisy gulped.

"Speaking of which, my mother is throwing a party in Kolt's honor Saturday. A sort of welcome to the family, ten-year catch-up on birthdays and Christmases. My parents didn't want to invite you, but I insisted. After all, it's the neighborly thing to do."

SEATED ON HIS FOLKS' SOFA Saturday afternoon, Luke had mixed feelings watching his son open a mountain of gifts. On one hand, he was so proud of the well-mannered, funny, likeable little guy that he was about to burst. On the other, Luke realized he'd had nothing to do with how Kolt had turned out beyond donating some DNA.

The living room was so crowded not only with the Montgomery clan, but with relatives from his mom's side of the family that Daisy had been forced to the dining-room table. Watching her brought on a whisper of nostalgia for happier times. Blotting that out, however, was the screaming reality of what she'd done. He and Kolt might be pals, but would they ever have the bond a father and son should? When Luke thought of what Henry had done, rage seized him, but so did his inherent mistrust of Kolt's mom. At a time when she should've run straight to Luke, she'd run away from him as fast as she could.

As if feeling his stare, Daisy looked up. Their gazes locked. Their connection was so undeniably strong his stomach tightened. She half smiled and on autopilot, he smiled in return before hastily focusing his attention on his son.

The day wound on with ten flavors of birthday cakes and an assortment of Christmas pies. Kolt and all other kids present were on obnoxious sugar highs.

"Nice party."

Luke glanced up from his third piece of cake to find his efforts to avoid Daisy had failed. At least they were in the quiet kitchen. The last thing they needed was an audience. "Yeah, uh, Mom and Dad went all out. They're excited about finally being grandparents."

"If that was another subtle dig at me, again, I'm sorry. I get that my actions hurt an awful lot of people."

Ignoring her, Luke finished off his cake.

"Are things ever going to get back to normal between us?" She'd softened her voice, in the process filling him with an asinine desire to turn back the clock. If lives were road maps, how many wrong turns had it taken to land them in their current position?

"What do you consider normal?" Luke didn't mean to be cruel, but seriously, the woman had vanished for ten years, didn't bother telling him he had a son and now expected everything between them to be hunky-dory? "We don't even have a baseline for what normal would look like."

"For starters," Daisy said, "we could talk. Share a meal. Discuss our son's future."

"We could do all of that," he agreed, "but what's the point? It's not leading anywhere. Do you honestly think we even have a shot at being friends?"

Her complexion paled. "I-if that's the way you feel, I'll leave. I assume you won't mind giving Kolt a ride home?"

"Of course, I don't mind."

She gathered her purse and keys from the bench beside the back door. "Please, thank your parents for me. And tell Kolt I said goodbye and I love him."

"Aw, Daisy…" Damn if she didn't have him feeling bad.

"What?" She stood in the open door. Luke knew he should ask her to stay, but he didn't have it in him. Being polite just wasn't in the cards. But what was? Clearly, he couldn't maintain this level of animosity. For Kolt's sake, Luke would have to find middle ground. "Okay, then," Daisy said when he couldn't find words. "Maybe I'll see you tonight?"

"Yeah…maybe."

She cast him one last wounded look before leaving.

FROM THE PARTY, DAISY WENT to Reasor's for Doritos and Reese's Pieces and coffee ice cream. Nothing soothed an aching heart like a good movie accompanied by a junk-food buffet.

She was standing in the checkout line when a man said from behind her, "Hey, there, pretty lady. Long time no see."

The graveled tone gave her chills. She didn't want to turn to see Henry, but she also didn't want him for one second thinking she was afraid.

"Like that dress on you," he whispered as they moved ahead in line. "Makes a nice showing of those curves you used to love for me to touch."

"Back off," Daisy said, trying to keep her cool despite her runaway pulse, "or I'll scream for security."

"You won't do that, because if you did, everyone in the store would know what a dirty little girl you are."

Bile rose, stinging her throat. She wanted to scream, but her vocal cords had frozen. Panic seized her, flooding her limbs with concrete. *Run!* her every instinct screamed, but her body refused to comply.

"Ma'am? Excuse me, ma'am? Are you ready?"

The checkout clerk's prodding jolted Daisy from her horrifying past to the present.

"S-security," she managed. "Is there a store officer?"

The middle-aged woman cocked her head toward a uniformed guard standing alongside the ATM machine. "Yes, but what do you need him for?"

Daisy turned to point at Henry, report what he'd done, only he wasn't there. Had she imagined the whole thing? Hand to her temple, she tried to stop the store from spinning.

"Ma'am? You all right?"

"Y-yes. Fine." Daisy paid for her few groceries, then returned to the ranch. The entire drive, she kept one eye on the road and the other on the rearview mirror. Only when she'd locked herself safely inside the house did her pulse slow.

"Heavens, girl," her mother said from the sofa where she was curled up with a book. "You're as pale as a jar of marshmallow creme. Are you coming down with something?"

"Maybe," Daisy said, setting her groceries and purse on the floor.

"Where's Kolt?"

"He's still at the party. I've got a headache and didn't want to spoil his fun. Luke's bringing him by later."

Nodding, her mother asked, "How are things going with Luke?"

"Could be better. If you don't mind, I think I'll lie down." She'd almost reached the stairs when she couldn't hold back tears a second longer.

"Sweetheart, what's wrong?" Rising from the couch, Georgina pulled her into a hug.

Daisy wanted to keep all of the day's troubles to herself, but she'd tried that tactic before with less than stellar results. First, Daisy shared what had happened at her son's party. "I felt like a pariah. Like Luke's whole family hates me. I don't blame them, but what am I supposed to do? How can I ever make up for what I've done?"

"Give it time," her mother counseled, helping Daisy sit on the nearest step. "Right now, Luke's family is no doubt just as shocked as we were to learn Kolt's been around all this time. What they don't have is the love we all feel for you. Love makes forgiving come a little more easily."

Groaning, Daisy covered her face with her hands. "Unfortunately, Kolt's party was the high point of my day. I stopped by the grocery store and who should step up behind me in line? Henry."

Her mother lurched back. "He didn't threaten you, did he?"

Daisy shook her head. "Just said awful things."

"Like what?" With her mother's arms securely around her, Daisy told the worst, and felt surprisingly better for sharing her pain. When Daisy finished, Georgina said, "You should tell your brothers and Luke about this."

"Please, no. It's too humiliating."

"Honey," Georgina tucked Daisy's hair behind her ears, "you have to get it through your thick head that Henry's the one who has a problem—not you."

"I know. In counseling, I've been over that fact a hundred times. But seeing him—having him that close—" She shuddered.

"Please at least talk to Luke about all of this."

"Why? What good would that possibly do? Especially when he can't stand the sight of me."

"Sure about that?" Drawing Daisy in for another hug, Georgina said, "When you get to be as old as I am, you tend to want to get past the BS and straight to the heart of things. Want my opinion? I think Luke's problem is that he never stopped caring for you. You devastated him once when you left all those years ago. Now you've hurt him again. He wants to trust you, but you've proven yourself—in his eyes, anyway—not worthy. The trick is going to be proving to Luke that not only have you learned from your mistakes, but that you're willing to work through them to regain the special bond the two of you once shared."

For Daisy, knowing her mother was right didn't make the task ahead any easier.

"I'm not by any means suggesting you try getting romantically involved, but for Kolt's sake, you should at least be civil."

Daisy sighed. "You're preaching to the choir, Mom."

Georgina cracked a smile. "I don't need the whole choir to hear me—just you."

"YOU TWO HAVE FUN?"

As Luke rounded the backside of his Jeep, he saw Daisy rise from one of the front-porch rockers. In the waning light, the sound of cicadas rising and falling in the still air, the sweet scent of freshly-watered petunias lacing the yard, he could almost forget what she'd done.

"Mom!" Loaded down with a pile of presents tall enough to nearly block his sight, Kolt shuffled across the parking area. "Grandma Peggy and Grandpa Joe gave me the best party ever! I got so many toys and games I could open my own store!"

"That's awesome, sweetie." She left the porch to help their son with his load. "Let's put all of your new things on the dining-room table for now, then get you ready for bed. We'll sort through everything in the morning."

"But I wanna play with it tonight."

"Kolt," Luke said, coming up behind his boy with an equally impressive load, "how about grabbing more stuff from the car?"

"Okay." Kolt scampered back the way he'd just come.

"I'd like a minute alone with you," Luke said to Daisy once their son was out of earshot.

"Good. I'd like to talk to you, too."

"You first," Luke said, motioning for her to start.

"No, you." Daisy fingered the long braid hanging over her right shoulder.

"Luke," Kolt called from the Jeep. "I'm gonna need your help with my bike."

"Sure." Luke looked to Daisy. "Be right back."

She nodded.

By the time the bike was set free, along with the ten-year-old riding hell-bent for leather down the drive, Luke no longer knew what to say.

"Does it bother you that Kolt calls you by your first name?" Daisy stepped up behind him.

"I'd be lying if I said it didn't, but given the circumstances, I think it's for the best. When—if—the time comes that he feels comfortable enough to call me Dad is something for him to decide."

"Even when we were kids," Daisy said, "I remember you doling out wisdom. The perpetual mediator."

"This bothers you?" The sun had set and lightning bugs sparked over the tall grasses on either side of the mile-long drive.

"I used to envy that quality. The way our friends came to you for advice." Over and over she stroked her braid, as if petting it for comfort. Was she nervous? About their situation? Or him in general?

"Funny how despite all of those times I helped everyone else, now I'm the one needing guidance."

"Look how fast I can go!" Kolt whizzed by on the bike Luke's parents had bought.

"Dang, bud, you're flying!"

"Slow down," Daisy urged. "It's too dark to go so fast without a helmet."

"Is that a maternal thing?" Luke asked Daisy. "Seems like my mom used to do the same. Just when I was having the best time, she'd shoot me down."

"It's not my intention to be a happy-smasher," Daisy said, "only to keep Kolt safe long enough to grow into adulthood."

"Why'd you leave the party?" The question had been on Luke's mind all afternoon.

"Exactly why you'd think. Your family understandably hates me. I felt about as welcome as roaches at a picnic."

Scratching his head, Luke asked, "Isn't the saying 'ants at a picnic'?"

"You know what I mean."

"Yeah," he admitted. "I do." Was it wrong to want to mess with her? "I wanted you to stick it out, though. I wanted my folks to see you're not intimidated by a few glowering old biddy aunts."

"What if I am?" Head bowed, she said, "I ran into Henry today. All he had to do was say a few words and I froze—literally, froze."

"Watch me do a stunt!" The gas lamplights that came on automatically when it grew dark enough illuminated the drive just enough to make Kolt visible when he jumped a twig. "Cool, huh?"

"Pretty awesome," Luke called out.

Kolt jumped the twig again before racing off down the drive.

"With the 'ears' safely out of hearing distance, want to tell me more about your run-in with Henry?"

"Not really." Tilting her head back, Daisy gazed up at the stars. "It's a nice night, but I suppose I should get in the house and put Kolt to bed."

"After that?" Luke asked.

"Want to hang by the pool? Maybe share a glass of wine?"

Yes. Luke would've liked nothing better. But the fact remained that he and Daisy were no good for each other. Time and Daisy's actions had proven it.

"Sorry," he said, "but I need to get home. Horses should've been fed over two hours ago."

"Sure." Arms folded, lips pressed tight, she nodded. "I understand."

But did she? Despite their most recent kiss that'd rocked him to his core, she had to know he was right in staying away.

"Great. Then, ah, tell Kolt good night for me. We have a date for church in the morning, so I'll pick him up around nine."

"I'll have him ready."

"Please do."

Was this how the rest of their lives were going to be? Short, to-the-point answers to each other's needs in regard to their son? Luke hated it, but he knew that for his sanity, steering clear of Daisy was his most sensible path. "All right, then. See you in the morning."

Walking away from her when she looked so alone and forlorn was no easy feat. But Luke managed, and he knew he'd be all the better for it.

Chapter Nine

"Hurry, pumpkin." Daisy sifted through Kolt's sock drawer to find a pair of navy ones to go with his khaki pants and cobalt shirt and tie. "We don't want to be late."

"I don't want to go." Kolt sat on the foot of his bed. He had bare feet, his shirt was buttoned crooked and his cowlick had never been more pronounced. Adorable, but not exactly the perfect image she was sure Luke's mom wanted to present. "I've never been to church."

Would the piles of guilt ever lessen? "It's actually nice. Lots of pretty singing, and probably you'll get introduced to lots of your grandparents' friends who want to give you hugs."

"I don't want strangers hugging me."

Sighing, Daisy stood. "Put on your socks and shoes. I need to grab earrings."

"Why are you going?"

"Because I want to."

Fifteen minutes later, Daisy opened the front door to Luke. She wore white slacks and a pink blouse, and she'd curled her hair and taken extra care with her makeup.

"Good morning. Hope you don't mind, but I'd like to tag along."

"Um, sure." Luke cleared his throat. "You look great."

"Thanks. Kolt's almost ready. Just finishing a bowl of cereal."

"What kind does he eat?" He reddened. "Stupid question, huh? I find myself wanting to know everything about the little guy. He's fascinating. Like I want to count his fingers and toes, but I guess the bus left the station on that one."

"I am sorry," Daisy said, remembering all too clearly the moment she'd first held Kolt in her arms. Aside from the wonder of it, she'd felt very alone. "If it's any consolation, at his birth, I wished you were there."

Luke's expression hardened. "No. That's no consolation at all. Am I even listed as his father on his birth certifi—"

"Okay, Mom! I'm done!" Kolt raced into the living room from the kitchen. "Hey, Luke."

"Hey, yourself. You're looking good this morning. All the old ladies at church are going to want to kiss you."

Kolt made a face. "That's what Mom said. Do I have to go?" On his way out the door, Kolt kicked it. "We never went in San Francisco."

"It's good to try new things. Plus, they have donuts and strong black coffee. Puts hair on your chest."

Kolt made another face.

"Not even food bribes make you want to go?"

Fastening his seat belt, Kolt shook his head.

"I suppose if it's all right with your mom, we could

skip church and catch up on chores around the house. Get down and dirty. Muck a few stalls." Luke put the car in gear and aimed it down the drive. "I've got a couple feed buckets with grain in them that need cleaning. They got wet during that rain we had the other night and I haven't had time to scrub 'em. The feed most likely soured. Might have a few maggots in it."

"I *love* maggots!" Kolt declared. "They sound way more fun than stupid church."

"What do you think, *Mom?*" The way Luke referred to her made Daisy inordinately happy. Truthfully, she'd enjoy nothing more than a lazy Sunday morning spent watching her guys work. "Sounds like a great idea. You get out of being kissed and hugged and Luke gets chores done. It's a win-win."

Especially for her!

"Only what would you think, bud, if we leave your mom here. I don't think she'll be much good to us if we're doing man work."

"Yeah," Kolt said as Luke backed up the Jeep. "Mom doesn't do good dirty work."

"If it's all right with you," Luke said to Daisy, "after we finish up, I'll probably take Kolt over to my folks' for Sunday lunch."

"Um, sure," Daisy said past the lump in her throat. Was Luke really so opposed to spending time with her even in a casual, family-oriented way? Opening her door when Luke pulled up to the porch stairs, she gave the guys as cheerful a wave as she could muster, considering she'd just been voted out of their club. "Have fun."

"We will!" Kolt was already diving for the front seat as Luke drove away.

For the longest time Daisy stood there, watching them go, trying to convince herself she wasn't feeling stuck in a pit of gloomy despair.

So what if her boys didn't want to be with her? She was already dressed for church, so she'd tag along with her mother. Then they'd have a gloriously civilized lady's lunch. And then, nice and full from far too many carbs, Daisy would fling herself across her bed and cry herself to sleep.

"LOOKS GOOD," KOLT'S DAD SAID, nodding at the lawn the boy had just mowed, "but you've got some clumpy parts that need to be raked."

"I've never raked in my life," Kolt whined. "And it's hot."

"Yup." While Kolt worked on the lawn, his dad got to have all the fun with the hose and maggots. "The rake's hanging on the barn tool rack. Grab it when you put the mower back where it goes. That wheelbarrow alongside the front porch would be a good place for you to put the grass clippings. Then you can dump it all in the compost bin."

"You're making me into a slave."

"You'll survive. When I was your age, I had to mow a yard twice this size every week."

When Kolt got back from the barn, it was like a million degrees hotter. He drank some of the ice water his dad had brought out, but it didn't help much in cooling him off. "Did your dad help?"

"Nope," Luke said. "The whole thing was my responsibility. It was tough, but when I finished, it felt good seeing it look so nice. Once you figure out how doing chores is actually important instead of boring, they won't seem so hard."

"I don't even know what that means." The rake was about eighteen cajillion feet taller than Kolt and he kept accidentally hitting himself in his leg. The spiky parts hurt.

"It means one of these days, when you have a family and house of your own, you'll be glad you learned how to do all of this stuff."

"Oh." Kolt supposed that made sense. Not that he ever wanted to get married, because girls were just gross. "Luke?"

"Yeah?" his dad answered, using a second rake to work alongside him.

"Did you want a kid?"

"Very much. Ever since I grew up, I've wanted a son. That's why I was sad that your mom kept you a secret."

"I know." Kolt rested his forehead on the rake's handle. "I don't get why she didn't just tell me about you when I was a baby. And now she says I have to stay away from Henry and that Uncle Dallas kicked him off the ranch. But that doesn't seem right. He was nice to me."

"Maybe so." His dad didn't take a break. "But I'm pretty sure you need to follow her directions. People aren't always as nice as they seem."

"Okay." Not wanting to look like a lazy little kid,

Kolt had raked and raked until his arms felt as if they were falling off. Uncle Dallas and Cash said it was good to work hard, and Kolt wasn't really sure why, but a squeezy feeling in his stomach made him want his dad to know he always did his best.

"How about a drink of water?" His dad held out the jug and Kolt took a long gulp. "Looks like we're about done here. Ready to move on to something else?"

"Can we brush the horses?"

"They don't need that right now," Luke said after taking another drink for himself, "but their stalls need cleaning. Would you help with that?"

"I guess. But brushing's more fun." Kolt followed his dad into the barn where they traded rakes for pitchforks and a wheelbarrow.

"True," his dad said, "but this is just as important."

After a long time while they were both just quiet and working, Kolt said, "On TV, dads seem more like they know what they're doing. How come you seem like you're not always sure?"

Luke laughed. "How could I be? We hardly know anything about each other. I don't know your favorite color or foods or even which football team you like."

"I like basketball better than football."

"There you go." Luke sat on a pile of hay bales, leaning forward to rest his elbows on his knees. "That's a perfect example. If I knew you better, I'd know stuff like that. Just like you'd know I love football, but only if the Sooners are playing. Want to go to a game with me this fall?"

"Sure."

Once they'd finished and gone inside to clean up to go to Luke's parents, Kolt stood on the front porch, waiting for Luke to get his cowboy hat. The just-mowed yard smelled nice. Looked nice, too. So did the barn. Kolt wasn't ready to tell anyone, but standing out here by himself, looking at how pretty everything was, he kind of understood what his dad had meant about how chores made you feel good inside. Kind of like when he made high grades at school.

"Ready?" Luke asked, slapping his hat on his head.

"Uh-huh."

Once they were in the Jeep, Kolt asked, "Do you think it would be all right if, after lunch, we get me a hat like yours?"

His dad gave him a long, kind of funny look, then nodded. "I think that'd be real nice."

A WEEK LATER, LUKE FOUND HIMSELF on the front lawn of Weed Gulch Elementary for his son's first day of fifth grade. For seven-fifty in the morning, the temperature was already climbing.

"This is embarrassing," Kolt said, shooing Daisy away when she stepped in close for her annual first-day-of-school snapshot. "Stop!"

"Just one more," she promised, pressing down his cowlick. "Luke, stand next to him. I want one of you both."

"Mom, please..." When a group of three older boys walked by, Kolt grew even more upset.

"What's wrong with you?" Daisy asked. "You used to love having your picture taken."

"I know," he said, messing up his hair, "but that was back when I was a baby. Now that I'm old, I can't do stuff like this anymore."

"Okay." She took one more candid shot. "I'm done."

"You've got both of our cell numbers if you need us, right?" Luke asked.

"Yes! Leave me alone." He ran off toward the entrance.

"What's the procedure now?" Luke asked.

Daisy said, "I generally walk him in, and make sure he gets settled. We met his teacher a few days ago when I picked up his supply list, so I don't especially need to see her again, but it's always good to sign up for PTA or find out if the class needs room moms."

"How about dads?" Luke might be new to the whole elementary-school scene, but he wanted in on everything. He'd already missed so much of his son's life. He wouldn't be absent a second more.

"Sure. Back in San Francisco, Kolt attended private school, but most parents were involved."

Inside, it didn't take long for Luke's eyes to adjust. What took longer was getting used to dozens of pint-size bodies darting like atoms through the halls.

Aside from a fresh paint job and new bulletin boards, the place didn't look all that different from when he and Daisy and all of her brothers had attended. It even smelled the same. Like dirty sneakers and super-strength cleaning solution.

"This is a trip, isn't it?" Daisy led the way to Kolt's room. "Seems like just yesterday when we were here."

"You were the hottest little third-grader I'd ever seen," he admitted. "Those braids of yours drove me wild."

"Stop," she said with a giggle.

They waved at Dallas's wife, Josie, who was a kindergarten teacher, and then stepped into Mrs. Olsen's room.

Cheerful rainbows hung from the ceiling and on the walls grew a paper garden with all of the girls' names written on flowers and the boys' on snails, frogs and squirrels.

The desks had been arranged in five groups of four and potted ivy, goldfish and a hamster lined the windowsill. The scent of fresh orange slices was a vast improvement over the odor in the hall.

Kolt stood with two other boys, one taller than him and one shorter. All of them had their supplies spread across the desks and from the looks of it were trading pencils.

"Does Kolt have cool pencils?" Luke asked, surprised to find his pulse racing, hoping his kid was well liked. Suddenly Luke's own issues were no longer important. In a remarkably short time, Kolt had become his world.

Daisy whispered, "Transformers were the best Dollar General had."

"Next year, we're going to Tulsa."

She elbowed him. "I'd hate to see what you'd do if we ever had a girl." The minute the words left her mouth, she covered it. "That came out wrong. I know we'll never have another baby. The two of us. Maybe apart. Hopefully…well—I'm going to shut up."

"I get it, Daisy." Luke knew what she was saying and in another world, one where she had never left and he had never had his heart broken by her, her sentiment might have come true. But no matter how special sharing this occasion with Kolt may be, it was all Luke and Daisy would ever have.

Kolt caught sight of them and waved them away.

"Come on," Luke said, hand on Daisy's upper arm. Just touching her triggered a wave of overwhelming need, but he ignored it. That was the sex talking. An area in which they'd never had a problem. A fact proven by the kiss he'd given her not too long ago. "Let's leave the kid alone."

"First, tell me you know I didn't mean what I just said. I was kidding."

"Lord," he said, raking his fingers through his hair, "this is neither the time nor place. Leave it alone."

"I can't." Tears had pooled in her eyes. Had he been a weaker man, they might've been his undoing. "I want you back in my life—as a friend—and for starters, I'm willing to take your smallest scraps."

"Stop." In the hall, with what felt like half the town streaming around them, he said, "You're stronger than this. Begging doesn't suit you."

"I need you to know I'm willing to do whatever it takes, for however long, to earn back your trust."

"I get that, but…" He looked away. At the next room over, a little girl clung to her father, crying that she didn't want him to go. A pang shot through Luke. A fear that the man would never be him. Would Kolt ever want to give him a hug? Would Luke one day experience the joy of being a father from the start of a child's life? "Trust isn't easy to come by, Daisy. It's not a tangible item to be picked up at the store. Once gone, sometimes it never comes back."

Raising her chin, sporting a look of defiance he hadn't seen since she'd bought her first bottle of Jack Daniel's, she said, "Get over yourself, Luke. I'm not asking you to marry me. Just to be my friend." Raising her hands only to slap them at her sides, she said, "Honestly, would that be so hard?"

"In a word—yes." Because if he were to surrender himself to her again, only to have her turn away, Luke feared he might never recover.

Chapter Ten

"Thank you so much." Daisy's new client, Jane Richmond, had tears in her eyes while leaving the office. A domestic violence victim, she'd finally summoned the courage to leave her abusive husband, but didn't know how to get him to pay child support. Daisy had filed the proper papers and gotten the legal ball rolling to get the guy in court. "I'm not sure how I'll ever repay you."

"That's the beauty of a free legal clinic," Daisy said with a hug. "All you have to worry about is caring for those adorable children. No guarantees, but I'll stay on Brian for as long as it takes to get what your babies are entitled to."

After more hugging and tears, Jane left.

Since Daisy's ad for free legal services had appeared a week earlier, Jane had been her only meaty case. She'd also done a couple of wills, helped mediate a land dispute and filed a few small claims court issues.

Since Luke's declaration on Kolt's first day of school, Daisy's pride had kept her away. While she appreciated her mother's advice on the matter of earning back his trust, clearly he more closely resembled a stubborn old mule than a man. As such, Daisy had decided to put her energy into helping people who wanted her in their lives.

As for Luke, he was a lost cause.

Another executive decision she'd made was to move out of the family home. As much as she loved being around her mother and Dallas and his wife and kids, she knew it was time for her and Kolt to get their own place.

The only foreseeable problem was Henry. She'd done some quiet investigating only to find he was still in the area, bunking with friends. On the ranch, Daisy felt reasonably safe. Though they didn't have security beyond the nightly alarm they set at the house, she reasoned there was safety in numbers. Henry would be foolish to mess with her when there were so many potential witnesses. On the other hand, he'd approached her in a crowded grocery store. Which told her if the man truly wanted to get to her, he'd find a way.

That said, Daisy refused to live one more day hiding in fear. She'd exiled herself for ten long years and had had enough.

At three o'clock, she waited until after weaving through school traffic before asking Kolt, "What do you think about looking at houses with me?"

"Why? We live at the ranch." He unwrapped a sucker he'd been given for acing his spelling test and popped it in his mouth.

"I know, but wouldn't it be nice to have a place of our own? You wouldn't have to share a bathroom with the twins and no more fighting over movies."

"I guess." Making a paper airplane from his candy wrapper, he asked, "Would Uncle Cash and Aunt Wren come over with Robin?"

"Sure. Everyone would be welcome to visit whenever they want." She stopped at the train crossing where the ringing signal brought on a headache.

"Luke said someday we could build a tree fort. Think the new house would have a spot for one?"

"I don't see why not." The train had to be eight miles long.

"Cool. He'll have to go with us to look, though. I don't wanna accidentally buy a house that wouldn't have a good tree fort tree."

Come on, train. "The two of us should be just fine on our own. I'm sure Luke wouldn't want anything to do with house-shopping."

"Sure he would, Mom. Let's call."

Before Daisy could stop him, Kolt picked up her cell and dialed Luke's phone.

"This is the last thing I thought I'd be doing today." Luke had just returned from a week-long stay at a ranch west of Oklahoma City and had looked forward to spending his Saturday loafing as much as possible. Instead, he was crammed into the backseat of a Realtor's Prius alongside the one woman he didn't want to be with.

Kolt sat in the front because he'd gotten carsick.

While Kolt and Vera discussed their favorite Disney Channel shows, Daisy said under her breath. "Trust me, I don't want you here just as much as you don't want to be here. If you hadn't told Kolt so much about how great it is building a tree fort, we wouldn't be in this predicament."

Predicament? More like torture. With the late August temperatures over a hundred, Daisy had worn a sundress. The damned thing not only displayed more creamy thigh than he could handle, but the effort it took to avoid the view down her collar was monumental.

"Here we are," Vera said, parking in front of the old Peterson place. Not only was it in desperate need of a paint job, but also a new porch, windows and roof. Had the dye on Vera's platinum hair sunk into her brain? "Six bedrooms and one bath. The kitchen needs updating and last time I was here we had to shoo out a squirrel, but aside from that, have you ever seen so much charm in a classic Victorian? As an added bonus, the acreage adjoins Buckhorn land."

Finally on his feet, it took Luke a good minute to stretch out the kinks.

While Vera and Kolt navigated crooked porch steps, Luke leaned in close to Daisy, "This is a joke, right?"

"I kind of like it. I've always loved this house. The turrets fascinated me. Aren't you excited that we get to go inside?"

Not really. "Just for a second, put aside any romanticism you might have for the old girl. Have you for one second considered how long the renovation would take? Not to mention, the cost?"

"Quit being a Debbie Downer and zip it." Cautiously following her son's path, she added, "The only reason you're even here is because of the whole tree fort thing."

"Yeah, well, if you buy this monstrosity, you might as well be living in a tree." Why'd she have to smell so good? The flowery scent distracted him from further discussion of the house's flaws. When her heel poked through a floor board, Luke was further bothered by having to catch her perfectly rounded derriere.

"Oops." Clinging to him, her cheeks flushed. "Thanks for the save. Guess that plank needs to be replaced."

"You think?"

"After J. T. Peterson died at the ripe old age of 101," Vera said in the living room, standing in front of a spectacular carved mantel, "the house sat vacant for ten years. Last year, the family tried renting it, but with no central heat or air, that didn't go so well."

The ceilings rose a good twelve feet and the entry-hall staircase beat anything Luke had seen, the way it hugged the oval room in a gentle rise. Though the house was no doubt infested with termites, mice and more than a few ghosts, it would really be something if it were ever to be restored—by, he hoped, anyone other than Daisy.

Upstairs, the bedrooms featured all manner of kooky angles to accommodate turrets and cupolas and stained-glass bays. The hardwood floors were in crappy condition. In many areas the ceiling looked as if it were caving in. The whole place reeked of dust and mildew and judging by Daisy's enraptured expression, she'd already made her decision.

"Mom! Look!" Kolt had found another winding staircase, this one leading to an attic that ran the full length of the house. Dormer windows allowed for plenty of natural light. "Have you ever seen so much cool stuff?" He'd found a chest filled with books and old clothes. Slapping a bowler hat on his head, he asked, "Do I look old-timey?"

"Absolutely," Daisy said. "Anything in there for me?"

He fished out a sailor's cap. "How's this?"

"Perfect," she said with a breezy smile Luke hadn't seen in years. "How do I look?"

"Okay, I guess—for a mom." She stuck out her tongue at their son.

"I want one." Luke mounted the last few steps. "No fair you two having all the fun."

"All that's left is this." Kolt tossed Luke a pillbox hat covered in torn netting and sporting a limp feather.

"Gee, thanks."

"Put it on!" Kolt demanded. "Mom can take a picture with her phone."

Laughing as the three of them squeezed together, Daisy stood in the center, extending her arm to snap the picture.

"Let me see." Kolt grabbed the phone. "Awesome! We look cool!"

"What a nice family you all make," Vera noted, popping her head above the railing. If only the newcomer to Weed Gulch knew of their rocky past, she wouldn't have been so quick to judge. "What do you think of the house?"

"I love it," Daisy said, "but I am daunted by all the work."

As she should be. But Luke remembered the fun he'd had fixing up his cabin. It hadn't been in much better shape, although it was considerably smaller, and the project hadn't been quite so massive in scale. Truthfully, he was a little jealous. For all its flaws, the home would one day be quite a jewel.

Vera waved off Daisy's concerns. "I'll hook you up with the names of dozens of reliable contractors. Besides, the heirs are pushing for a quick sale. This is the perfect time to get a lowball offer through."

"HAPPY?" LUKE ASKED. Daisy had signed her offer papers and they now sat at Lucky's Diner. While Daisy finished her BLT, Luke worked on the roast beef special. Kolt was long gone; he'd run into a friend from school at the Realtor's office, and Jonah's mother had taken him to their house to play.

"I am." Dredging her fry in ketchup, she said, "I need a project."

"Thought that's what your legal clinic was?"

"It is, but that occupies my days." Swirling artificial sweetener into iced tea, her expression turned wistful. "The house will give me something to do nights and weekends. Don't take this as a thinly veiled plea for your companionship, but I get lonely. After Kolt goes to bed, there's only so much reading and toenail-painting a girl can do."

He wouldn't admit it, but Luke understood. Many a night he'd spent on his front porch, staring out at the view, wishing for a woman to share it with. Only, so far, no one even close to suitable had come along. He could thank Daisy for that. "What about your mom and sisters-in-law? Aren't they good company?"

"Sure, but once conversation turns to babies or marriage, I feel like a third wheel. Other than our last names, we have nothing in common."

Finishing off his potatoes and gravy, Luke asked, "How's a house supposed to keep you company?"

Her expression flashed annoyance. "What it's going to do is keep me so busy, I won't have time to think about much else."

"Is that healthy?"

Forehead furrowed, she asked, "Is it any of your business?"

"In a roundabout way. I'd like to see Kolt's mom happy and normal. I don't want my kid growing up with a head case."

Pushing back her plate, she rested her forearms on the table. "Who appointed you Mister Perfection? I mean, seriously, you're always preaching about how untrustworthy I am and now, you just assessed me as borderline insane?"

"I did not." He downed the last of his sweet tea. "You're being a drama queen."

"Takes one to know one."

"What?" He wanted to lob another verbal weapon, but her childlike comment was such a blast from the past, all he could do was smile.

"You heard me." She smiled, too. "Sorry. I'm not sure where that came from. What were we fighting about?"

"I don't even remember."

"Perhaps that's a sign," she teased. "You're too serious."

"Me?" Hands to his chest, he said, "Mom's all the time nagging me to get a real job. Settle into a serious relationship. Seems to me you're the one needing help in that department. After all, who just bought a house in need of eight million bucks worth of repair?"

She tossed her wadded napkin at him. "It won't be anywhere near that expensive and nice try at changing the subject." She leveled a look at him. "You're a great-looking guy, have a good job—despite what your mother thinks—why haven't you remarried?"

"Lord, Daisy, do we have to get into this? You're giving me indigestion." The diner, with its yellow walls, faded linoleum floors and mismatched booths was usually one of his favorite places in town to hang out, but tonight, it felt uncomfortably warm. "Besides, I could easily flip your question around to ask it of you. You're hot, loaded, educated—a total package. Who wouldn't want what you have to offer?"

"Hmm…" Tapping her finger on her lips, she said, "You. On more than one occasion, you've made it clear I'm less attractive to you than your average ordinary leper."

"That's not fair. You know exactly why we'll never be together."

"Do I?" She glanced over her shoulder to find the booth behind her empty before whispering, "Because that kiss you gave me in my office made me think different. That maybe we just need to explore possibilities."

"Are you coming on to me?" In another lifetime, he'd have taken her straight out to his backseat, but now, there was just no way.

"Why would I do that? Especially when you want nothing to do with me? However, isn't that Rowdy Clements from Dallas's graduating class up at the counter? I haven't talked to him in ages." Taking a twenty and a five from her wallet, she left it on the table, then stood. "Maybe he'll want to talk to me? Bye."

"Sit your sweet behind back down," Luke practically growled. "Everyone in town knows Rowdy's a two-timing lowlife out for nothing but a good time."

"What a coincidence—so am I." She winked before sashaying right on over to the counter bar.

With everything in him, Luke longed to toss Daisy over his shoulder, but what kind of message would that send? In no way did he have any claim to her. No use sending out signals he wanted that to change.

Even if a small part of him did.

"Honey, you can't be serious?" Georgina wasn't exactly thrilled with the news of Daisy's anticipated purchase. "That old ruin was sagging when I had you. I can't even imagine what it must look like now. For heaven's sake, the yard is so overgrown, you can't even see the house from the road."

"I know," Daisy said, placing the folder with her paperwork on the kitchen counter. "But that's part of its beauty. I'll be saving the home for future generations."

Dallas snorted. "Ask me, you'd be better off throwing money in a fire."

"I didn't ask you," Daisy snapped. "Why can't all of you be excited for me? Not only is it a lovely historic home, but the forty acres adjoin our land. If for no other reason, Dallas, I would've thought you would be the first person in line with an offer."

"I was. The family got wind of the fact that I planned to doze the place and turned me down."

"I'm glad."

"Both of you hush." Georgina put the tomato she'd been cutting on top of chopped salad greens. "If I didn't know better, I'd swear you were both back in kindergarten."

Josie, who'd been sitting at the kitchen table writing lesson plans, cleared her throat. "Point of fact—my kindergartners are better behaved."

"Way to stand up for the man you supposedly love." Dallas kissed his wife.

"Oh—I love you, I just think you're being short-sighted. Daisy, if you ever need help, please give me a call. I love painting and decorating."

Daisy brushed Dallas out of her way to steal a hug from his wife. "Consider yourself hired."

"When do you find out if your offer is accepted?" Georgina asked, placing the salad at the center of the kitchen table.

"Hopefully tonight, but you never know."

"Well, regardless of the outcome," Georgina said, "we'll support you. Although, I'd rather do yard work than anything inside."

Daisy hugged her mom, too. "Great. Thanks. All right, Dallas, you're the only one without a job."

He scoffed at her suggestion. "Count me out. Someone needs to maintain this house so when my sister loses her shirt on this deal she has somewhere to live."

AFTER THE DINNER DISHES had been washed and put away, Kolt had come home from Jonah's, taken his bath, brushed his teeth and gone to bed, and Daisy once again found herself dreading the empty hours remaining in the day.

Dallas and Josie were holed up in their room, watching TV. Every so often, their laughs punched through the silence.

Georgina was in her craft room, working on a Christmas quilt.

Daisy, meanwhile, sat on the foot of her bed, pouting because she hadn't received her much-anticipated real-estate call.

When her cell chose that moment to ring, her heart leaped to her throat. Expecting Vera, hearing Luke came as a surprise.

"Did you get the house?" he asked.

"I don't know." Tossing back her covers, she climbed in, propping pillows behind her. "Do you think it's a bad sign they haven't already called?"

"Not necessarily."

"That didn't sound overly confident." Nibbling her lower lip, she imagined him seated in his comfy armchair. He'd wear PJ bottoms and nothing else. Suddenly overheated, she pushed back her down comforter.

"All I'm saying is they could be out of town or working late. Maybe their phone's broken. You never know."

"I suppose you're right." Hearing his rich, country twang directly in her ear did delicious things to her insides. "Funny, but before I saw that house, I wasn't even sure I wanted my own place. Now, it's all I can think about. I'm ready to jump out of my skin."

"How'd your date go?"

"What date?" She sat up straighter. Was he talking about Rowdy? She'd forgotten even talking to him. Turns out he'd been waiting for his latest girlfriend, so they'd spent three minutes chatting and then Daisy had left. End of story.

Luke laughed. "You don't have to play coy with me. I'm not the jealous type."

"Why would you be? Especially when you've told me how little I mean to you."

"I never said that," he protested. "Obviously, I care about you or I wouldn't have called."

"Mmm-hmm." Should Daisy be flattered by his concern?

"How's Kolt?"

"Nice change of topic, but for the record, he finished his homework and is tucked into bed."

"Think he could spend the night over here some time? I'd like that—helping him with his routine." Luke's question struck Daisy in a long-forgotten place. It took her mind off the potential house deal and all the petty bickering she and Luke had shared. In the end, this was the sentiment at the core of Luke's pain. He'd missed not only countless Christmas programs and soccer games, but more importantly, the little times. The quiet moments like bedtime stories and sweet, heartfelt prayers.

"Of course," she said past the knot in her throat. "For that matter, once we're settled in the new house, there's plenty of room for you to hang out there as much as you'd like. No pressure—just putting the offer on the table."

"Thank you." The warmth behind his words struck her as different from his usual tone—at a level it hadn't been at in a very long time.

"Sure, Luke. I'll do whatever you need in order for you and Kolt to grow close."

He stayed silent for a long while. "I hope you get your house, Daisy."

"I appreciate that." He had no idea how much.

"Well…" He laughed. "Guess I should let you go."

"Yeah. I have, um, stuff to do." Liar. If Daisy had her way, she'd have curled up in her bed, chatting with him for hours. She liked the rich timbre of his voice. The way he'd made her loneliness disappear.

"Me, too."

"Okay…" *You hang up first, because I'm not strong enough to sever this tenuous tie.*

He laughed again, this time slowly and sexily enough to make her stomach tighten. "Good night, Daisy. Sweet dreams."

When he hung up, for a moment she felt lost. Then she remembered that when it came to Luke, she'd never even been found.

Chapter Eleven

"Congratulations," Vera said early the next morning. "My sellers accepted your offer."

"Eek." Daisy did a happy dance in her office desk chair. Considering the amount of work she had ahead of her, she should've been terrified, but all she could focus on was the end result of raising Kolt in such a grand old home.

"I'll be over this afternoon with final documentation, and even though we already know of a few existing trouble spots, I still recommend getting a professional inspection for possible foundation issues."

After settling on a time to meet, Daisy tried concentrating on the few projects Barb had sent her way, as well as several more pro bono cases she'd taken, but she had a hard time concentrating when all she really wanted to do was start scraping and painting.

She called her mother to share the news, and then Wren and Josie.

Kolt would have to wait until after school.

As for the one person she most wanted to tell, Daisy knew she shouldn't call Luke. Every time she spoke to him it was akin to ripping off a bandage a tiny bit at a time. He meant so much to her, but she wasn't entirely sure why. Yes, they'd been the quintessential high-school sweethearts and shared a child, but beyond that, they were strangers. He knew nothing of her dreams or goals and she didn't know his.

So why was it that whenever he was near—as he'd been the day they'd been out house-hunting—she was constantly checking herself to make sure she hadn't inadvertently brushed against him or too often said his name?

Exhausted from overanalyzing every little thing in her life, Daisy pushed back her chair and stood at one of the windows overlooking the town's busiest street.

All seemed normal in Weed Gulch, so why did she feel uneasy? Expectant? Maybe she shouldn't have put an offer in on the house?

There she went again, second-guessing. But why? Why couldn't she accept her lot in life and be happy?

With all of her secrets finally in the light of day, with Henry, she hoped, far, far away, at times her overall satisfaction meter felt unbearably full. Other days, the weight of what, in Luke, she hadn't lost but had practically given away, felt crushing. The trick was not dwelling on the past. She had Kolt and the rest of her family, and a dilapidated house that might as well be a second child.

Deciding fresh air might help her mood, Daisy powered down her computer, grabbed her purse and keys and locked up.

Outside, she winced at the bright sun.

The heat blasted her as if she'd stuck her head in an open five-hundred-degree oven.

She climbed into her car, only to be that much hotter.

Damn, this stupid weather. When she'd talked to Barb that morning, she'd reported it raining and seventy-five degrees. Should she back out of her house deal and just go home? Would San Francisco still feel like home?

Arching her head back, she groaned, only to have an image in the rearview mirror catch her eyes.

On the back window, someone—no doubt, Kolt—had scrawled:

I See You.

Grinning, she started the engine and backed out of the lot. All of her worries were unfounded. What she needed to do was relax and fully embrace this new chapter in her life. As for Luke... Daisy had no choice but to be satisfied without him.

WEED GULCH GOSSIP had it on good authority that Daisy had gotten her house. On that evidence, Luke had stopped by Reasor's for a big bunch of flowers and was now headed up the Buckhorn Ranch main drive.

In all the years he'd known the family, he'd rarely knocked before entering and this time was no exception.

"Hello?" he called once inside.

When no one answered, he followed the sound of laughter and found the whole clan grilling hamburgers by the pool. Just as he had when facing the prospect of Daisy moving into her new house without him, Luke felt irrationally slighted by not having been invited to the cookout.

Forcing a smile, reminding himself this was a place where he'd always been welcome even without a formal invite, Luke asked the chef, "Is it too late to get mine medium-rare?"

"Long time no see," Dallas said, backing up when fat from the meat caused the gas flame to flare.

"Cooking burgers or your facial hair?"

"Little of both," Josie teased, slipping her arm around Dallas's waist, "just think of it as bonus protein."

"I'll try."

As much as Luke enjoyed horsing around with his old friend, he searched the back porch and pool area for Daisy and his son.

"Looking for someone?" Dallas asked, a smile lighting his eyes.

Luke tossed the flowers on the table. "Nope. Just you."

"I'm flattered. But in case you have a hankering to see my sister and nephew, they're upstairs, getting into their swimsuits. Wanna borrow trunks?"

"Sure." Had Dallas noticed Luke's relief? Why, Luke couldn't say, but lately he'd craved Daisy and his son more than his favorite brand of ice cream sandwich. "Your mom still keep a bunch of them in the pool house?"

"You know it."

A few minutes later, Luke ditched his jeans and

T-shirt to step onto the diving board he hadn't played on in years.

"Cannonball!" Dallas shouted from the grill.

"Don't you dare!" Daisy called from the shallow end. "I don't want wet hair."

As a kid, Luke would've ignored Daisy's wishes, going so far as to get her as wet as possible. But as a grown man, he dove cleanly into the tepid water, surfacing with barely a splash feet from where she stood. "Hey."

"Hey, yourself."

Just looking at her, he couldn't help but smile. She'd piled her hair high in a messy bun, and still had curves in all the right places. Her black bikini didn't leave much to the imagination. "Remember the last time we went swimming?"

"Shh," she admonished, cheeks flaming. "You promised never to speak of that again."

"But it was fun."

"Luke!" Kolt rocketed out of the French doors. "We're having a barbecue party 'cause we got our new old house. You wanna have hamburgers with us? I told Mom we should ask you, but she said you probably wouldn't wanna come."

"This true?" Luke asked his son's mom.

Daisy focused on retrieving the beach ball floating nearby. "I know you're busy."

"Never too busy for a party."

She rolled her eyes. For his ears only, she asked, "Do you intentionally send out such mixed signals, or is toying with me your favorite game?"

"What are you talking about?" Her question genuinely confused him.

"The way one minute you're shamelessly flirting, and the next, telling me how we don't stand a chance even as friends."

"I wasn't flirting," he protested, slicking the water back from his hair. "Hell, I wouldn't even know how."

"You are so full of yourself." She whisked her hand over the water just hard enough to give him a light splash.

Jumping back, he warned, "Watch it. For a woman wanting her hair to stay dry, you're playing with fire."

"Mom!" Kolt hollered from the diving board. "Watch me!"

Shielding her eyes from the sun, she called, "I'm watching, sweetie!"

Hopping on the end of the board, Kolt said, "Luke, you watch, too!"

"Okay, bud! Show me what you've got!"

Kolt's dive wouldn't land him in the Olympics any time soon, but Luke's chest swelled with pride all the same.

"That was great," he said when Kolt popped up from under the water. "You're really good."

"Thanks." Kolt beamed.

"Sweetie," Daisy said, "show Luke your fancy dive."

"Okay!" While Kolt repositioned himself for another show, Luke studied Daisy—the way her whole face fairly glowed, watching their son. For each year she'd been gone, she'd grown infinitely more beautiful.

"Hold on tight for this one," she advised. "It's a pretty awesome move."

Kolt ran off the board, giggling and wiggling. Any reputable judge would've scored him a zero. In Luke's eyes, however, his kid had earned a solid ten.

"You're amazing," Luke said when Kolt swam his way.

"Really think so?" Kolt asked.

"Absolutely. You'll need a pool at your new house so you can keep practicing your moves."

Kolt's reaction to the suggestion was to give Luke a huge smile and an ambush hug. "We'll put the pool right by our tree fort. You need to help me pick where they're gonna go."

With his son still clinging to him, for Luke, time slowed and then froze. Daisy grinned at him from where she sat on the pool steps and in that moment, Luke had never felt more complete. Yes, Daisy had screwed up royally by not immediately telling him she was pregnant, but was Luke prepared to toss away what could potentially be a great future all because of fear? If so, how was he any different from Daisy who had kept Kolt's existence from him for the very same reason?

"You two men look handsome together," she said.

"I don't know what you think," Luke said to Kolt, "but I'm thinking your mom is pretty gorgeous."

Kolt made a face. "You're not gonna kiss her, are you?"

"I hope not," Dallas said with an odd tone. "Because the burgers are done, meaning all of you slackers need to get out of the water."

All through dinner, Luke couldn't shake the feeling that his friend didn't approve of a potential rematch between him and Daisy.

When the ladies volunteered for KP duty, Luke seized the opportunity to ask Dallas what was on his mind. "Why do I get the feeling you're not a big fan of the idea of me and your sister giving things another shot?"

"Because I'm not." Dallas eased onto a chaise lounge, resting his arms behind his head. "Bet it's going to rain tomorrow. The knee I twisted in that ice storm a couple years back hurts like hell."

"Nice try at avoiding the issue," Luke said, sitting in the chair beside him, "but I would've thought you of all people would support a reunion."

"Used to think I would," Dallas said. "But after this business with Henry, Daisy's messed up. She'd have to be to keep you from your son."

"Yeah," Luke said. "I agree."

"Which proves my point." Dallas winced while repositioning his leg. "Seems to me you'd be better off going with someone new. So would Daisy. The two of you together?" Dallas shook his head. "Never work."

"You're pissing me off," Luke said, his whole body tensed. "I've known you my whole life. You know the kind of solid man I am. What makes you think for a second I couldn't make Daisy happy?"

Gazing across the glassy pool, Dallas said, "I don't for a second doubt that. What worries me is that you even have to ask. Used to be, when it came to Daisy, the two of you just did whatever you wanted. To hell with what anyone else thought. Now, you're too mechanical about it. For the sake of your son, I think part of you wants to be with his mom, do the whole perfect family routine, but wanting isn't enough. You have to need it. In here." He patted his chest.

Luke rolled his eyes. "Dallas the philosopher."

"Mark my words," his supposed friend said, "you go into a relationship for any reason but love, you're either going to get burned or light the fire. Either way, no one's getting out alive."

"Nice." Rising, Luke said, "Remind me next time I need a friend to look elsewhere."

"Don't say I didn't warn you."

After changing back into his jeans and T-shirt, Luke bypassed Dallas on his way into the house. He found Daisy putting leftover tomato and onion slices in a plastic container. Bonnie and Betsy sat at the kitchen table struggling with math homework. "Thanks for dinner," he said, "but I've gotta go feed my horses."

"Sure," she said. "Rub some noses for me."

"Will do. Where's Kolt?"

"Upstairs changing." Putting the tub in the fridge, she added, "He's got spelling words to practice."

Not entirely ready to leave, yet not sure what else to say, Luke nodded. "I, ah, got you flowers. They were on the table outside."

On her way to stash leftover buns in the pantry, Georgina said, "I wondered who those were from. I already put them in water."

"Thanks," Daisy said. Luke couldn't tell if she'd meant the sentiment for him or her mom.

"Thought you had to feed your horses?" Bonnie glared up at him.

"I do," Luke said. "What's with the mean look?"

"You ate the last scoop of potato salad and *everyone* knows that's my favorite." Hands on her hips, Bonnie resembled a pint-size linebacker, itching for a fight.

"Yeah," her twin, Betsy, chimed in. "*Everyone* knows."

Hands up, Luke said, "Sorry. Next time I won't take a single bite."

"Better not," Bonnie said with an extra-fierce scowl.

"Knock it off." Georgina gave both girls swats on their behinds in passing. "Daisy, why don't you walk our guest to his car."

Safely in the living room, Luke asked his escort, "They this territorial about other things?"

Laughing, Daisy said, "As far as I can tell, they don't like sharing cookies or deviled eggs, either. If you have a hankering for brussel sprouts, you should be safe."

"Good to know. Thanks for the intel."

Outside, serenaded by the cicadas' rise-and-fall song, Luke was again struck with the notion that he didn't want the night to end. His quiet cabin didn't hold its usual appeal.

"I never asked what brought you by," Daisy said.

"I heard through the grapevine that you got your house. Wanted to congratulate you."

"Oh. Thanks." Her faint smile contained layer upon layer of meaning Luke wasn't equipped to decipher. Why couldn't women be as easy to read as horses? "I was pretty jazzed."

He asked, "When do you close?"

"End of the week. For the deal I got, I'm paying cash from my trust. Without loans, it's a simple transaction."

Looking to his boots, then back to her, he asked, "Once you're in, think I might be able to help?"

"Sure." A light breeze caught her hair, floating it back from her face. Superhuman restraint was the only thing keeping Luke from grazing his fingertips along her cheeks to sweep those loose strands behind her ears. "Kolt and I will need every willing body we can find."

"Good. I want to be there—for both of you."

"While I'm grateful for the offer," Daisy said, "I'm also a little suspicious. What happened to your solid stance on staying away from me?"

Good question.

"Look," he said, hands crammed in his pockets, "I've never claimed to be perfect. Occasionally I say things I probably shouldn't. I'm not saying I'm ready to settle down with a white picket fence, but what could it hurt if we spend time together—like a family?"

"Don't..." Daisy's smile faded. "It's not fair for you to insert yourself into every aspect of our lives without commitment. Now that you're a part of Kolt's life, he'll expect you to stay."

"Which is exactly what I'm offering."

"No." She smacked her palm against the hood of his Jeep. "What you want is to play house, but I'm not interested. More than anything, I crave a lasting relationship, a man to hold me in the quiet of night, but

I'm not desperate. Not nearly ready to beg for a man's crumbs."

"You're being ridiculous." Taking his keys from his pocket, Luke rounded to the driver's side of the car. "First, I never offered anything—let alone, crumbs. Second, this has nothing to do with you and me, but with me and my son. I have a right to spend time with him."

"Of course you do." Tears pooling in her eyes told him he didn't have a right to toy with her heart. But he failed to see how hearts even entered into it. Was this one of those cryptic woman things?

"Thank your mom for dinner," he said.

Daisy crossed her arms as if hugging herself.

"Sharing Kolt doesn't have to be complicated," Luke said. "You're making a bigger deal out of it than need be."

"Just go." She turned away from him to wipe her eyes.

For the life of him, Luke couldn't figure what Daisy wanted. She was the one who'd left him. She'd kept his son a secret for ten years. From where he stood, he was the injured party.

"Please, Luke…"

Bracing his hands on the edge of the car's roof, he said, "I don't know what you want from me. I'm offering all I have to give."

Turning her back on him, she marched up the front porch stairs.

"Real mature, Daisy! We're having a conversation here!"

She entered the house and closed the door behind her, audibly ramming the dead bolt.

Luke kicked his tire.

Honestly, the woman hadn't matured one iota since turning fourteen. He was sorry for what Henry had put her through—more than he could ever adequately convey, but that didn't give her the right to play with him like this.

One minute, her smile put him on top of the world. The next, her pretty pout kicked him to the gutter. Where did that leave him? The last thing he needed was drama.

What *did* he need?

After this latest encounter with Daisy? A good, stiff drink.

Chapter Twelve

"No way are you and my grandson spending so much as a single night here until at least the roof is fixed." Friday afternoon, Georgina stood in the living room of Daisy's new home, decked out in rubber boots and gloves, looking as if her family were in danger of an imminent dust-bunny attack.

"I know," Daisy said, "I've already got a roofing contractor lined up." Ever since being handed the keys, Daisy felt as if someone had pressed Fast Forward on her days. She'd had so many new legal clients that some minor cases had had to be turned away. Barb was also keeping Daisy's work plate full. "They'll be working in conjunction with a preservation team I hired out of Tulsa. They specialize in reinforcing and bringing up to code the overall structure."

"Look at that crown molding." Josie craned her neck for a better view. "It'd cost a fortune to have that kind of craftsmanship nowadays."

"True." Georgina parked her bucket filled with warm, sudsy water in front of the mantel. "Thank heavens you don't have to strip all of this wood."

"Tell me about it." Daisy had her own bucket and was attacking baseboards. No doubt all of it would have to be scrubbed again after the carpenters did their thing, but it was satisfying to do work that made an immediate difference. With Kolt sleeping over with Jonah, the last thing Daisy needed was time for her mind to wander. "I think I'm going with a soft white for the trim, and then I'll have to look into finding reproduction wallpapers and paint colors."

"I had no idea you were even interested in this sort of thing," her mother said.

"I dated a guy in San Francisco who was a historic architect for the Landmarks Preservation Advisory Board. It's really fascinating how much behind-the-scenes effort it takes to keep a town's architectural history intact."

"Back up the train," Josie said, sitting on her heels. "This history lesson is exciting and all, but I want to spend more time on the guy. How serious did it get and do you still hear from him?"

Laughing, Daisy said, "After dating me, Marcus opened his closet door—if you know what I mean."

"No, I don't," Georgina admitted. "Oh, wait. *Oooh.*"

Josie and Daisy laughed.

"Anyway," Daisy continued, "I love him and his significant other to death and we're all Facebook and email buddies, but that's about the extent of our romance."

"Not to be a prying mother," Georgina said, "but what's going on with you and Luke? My gardening committee and I naturally assumed that with Kolt, you two would marry."

Daisy nearly choked on her own spit. "Tell me you seriously don't discuss things like that in public."

"Oh, please." Georgina waved off Daisy's concerns. "The whole town's talking about it. Just as everyone was shocked and upset about Henry, they're excited about the prospect of you and Luke finally getting your happily-ever-after."

"Please, Mom," Daisy urged, "if that's what you're hoping for, take it off your wish list. It's never going to happen."

"Why?" Josie asked. "You two are cute together. And Kolt's the spitting image of his father."

Daisy made a face. "True and true, but Luke's made it clear he has no intention of becoming an official part of my life."

"Georgina, cover your ears," Josie said.

"Fiddlesticks," Georgina complained, "I've been gossiping about boys since before you two were born."

Josie grinned. "Sorry. I was just going to ask if he's kissed you—you know, like recently? And if so, were there sparks?"

More like a flaming volcano! Daisy prayed the heat rising in her cheeks wasn't visible.

"I'm taking your blush to mean he *has* kissed you and it was amazing," Josie said. "So what's the problem?"

"He's a man," Georgina noted, "and my baby girl crushed his ego to the size of a pea. Now, he's scared that if he goes and messes up by falling for her again, Daisy's going to pull the same runaway stunt."

"Which is ridiculous," Josie pointed out. "She just bought a house. How much more permanent can a girl get?"

"Great point," Georgina said with a big nod.

"Excuse me," Daisy said, "but if you two let me get a word in edgewise, you'd understand that I don't even want Luke. I mean, sure, I'd like him around for Kolt, but he does nothing for me—you know, as far as the whole butterflies in the stomach thing goes. In fact Luke is—"

"Someone mention my name?" The beast strolled through the open front door.

Mortification didn't come close to describing Daisy's embarrassment level.

Georgina cleared her throat. "Luke, I was just commenting on how my daughter wrangled me into unpleasant household chores when all I promised in regard to this old relic was help in restoring the garden."

"And that's when your name came into the conversation," Josie said as a quick cover. "We thought you would be the perfect person to help Daisy with her project. Dallas is all the time saying how handy you are when it comes to fixing things around the house."

"Nice to know he thinks so highly of me," Luke said, tugging on the brim of his cowboy hat.

"Josie, hon…" With a grunt, Georgina pushed to her feet. "Would you be a dear and drive me over to Lucky's? I have a powerful craving for sweet tea."

"That does sound good," Josie said, already gathering her purse and keys. "Daisy, you going to be all right with your jug of ice water?"

Daisy shot her so-called loving family the dirtiest look she could muster. They thought they were playing Cupid, but in reality, they were only making her situation worse. She longed for a nice, comfortable friendship with Luke—that was all. She'd grown weary of bickering and just wanted peace.

Once Georgina and Josie left, Luke said with a slow, sexy grin, "You might look into hiring new help. Those two seem worthless."

"Tell me about it." Sitting on one of the collapsible camp chairs she'd brought, Daisy said, "If you stopped by to see Kolt, he's not here."

"Bummer." Luke removed his hat, hanging it on the newel post. "I'd hoped we could have a tree fort planning meeting."

"He would like that. I'm picking him up from Jonah's tomorrow at noon. Want to come back around one?"

"Sounds doable." Instead of returning his hat to his head, and then leaving, Luke stood around, fidgeting with this and that. He picked up a bottle of lemon oil, read the label. Took a few leaves that'd skittered from the porch through the open door, stashing them in a trash bin.

"Good." Grabbing the broom, Daisy avoided eye contact with Luke by working dirt from the nearest corner. "He'll enjoy spending time with you."

Luke had grown uncomfortably aware of how much he enjoyed the company of Kolt's mom. Had he one iota of smarts, he'd have long since been out the door.

Daisy glanced his way. In the process, hair escaped her ponytail, spilling into her eyes. In his mind, Luke stood next to her, sweeping it back, making her own escape an impossibility. He'd pin her into her corner, relishing the way he made her heart race as if she were a caged canary. She'd lick her lips. He'd sweep his hands from her cheeks, down her throat, her shoulders, her arms to land on her hips. Then he'd kiss her. Long and leisurely until she begged for more.

Had things between them not been so complicated, the afternoon might take on a whole new spin. As it was, he felt dirty for even thinking he wanted her. The two of them were over. What was his body's problem with understanding that message?

"I'll be sure and tell Kolt you stopped by." Dripping it all over the battered wood floor, she took her filthy wash water to the kitchen.

Luke knew better, but he trailed along behind her, liking the view until reaching the room that had last been renovated in the seventies and featured avocado everything.

Pushing himself up onto a dusty counter, he noted, "You do know all of your modern stuff from San Francisco is going to look like crap in here."

"Did I ask your opinion?" After pouring the dirty water in the sink, she filled her bucket with fresh water, this time opting for warm.

He shrugged. "Just saying…"

Daisy added a few capfuls of cleaner to her bucket. "Is there a specific reason you're still here? Other than to harass me?"

"Is that the way you think of me? As an imposition?" Why, he couldn't say, but the notion troubled him.

She sighed. "Honestly, I try not to think of you. You've made it clear how you feel about me and I'm making peace with that."

"Good. Great." Shoving his hands in his pockets, he nodded. "Glad we're on the same page."

From the front of the house came the sound of clomping footfalls on the porch.

"Hello?" Georgina sang out. "If y'all are thirsty, we brought sweet tea!"

Luke took that as his cue to exit.

He seriously needed to go on a date. Needed to work out his frustrations with a woman with whom he stood a chance in hell of going the proverbial distance.

"HEY, LUKE!" KOLT CALLED at the zoo Sunday afternoon.

Luke had originally planned to invite Daisy, but changed his mind. When it came to spending time with his son, Luke couldn't get enough, but lately, each time he and Daisy shared space they shared ugly words.

"Did you see how the mom chimp was looking at me?"

"What did you do to make her stare?"

"I was sticking out my tongue and jumping. Like this." Kolt did his best monkey imitation loud enough to startle a baby who'd been sleeping in her stroller.

The baby's mom gave Kolt a glare, but the chimp mother seemed unaffected by his performance.

"Hey, bud, take it down a notch." Luke guided his son from the building. "Hungry?"

"Nah. Let's look at more animals."

After winding their way through forest and swampland and even the petting zoo, Luke was beginning to think he'd gotten an Energizer Bunny instead of a kid.

In front of a giant rope spiderweb, Kolt called, "Let's climb that!"

Luke asked, "Do I have to?"

"Yeah! Come on!"

They'd climbed around for a while, with Luke finding web-climbing to be not so bad, when two teens strolled by hand-in-hand, doing more kissing than animal observation.

"That's gross," Kolt noted, nodding in their direction. "But my friend Jonah was talking about you and Mom and wondering why you're not, like, boyfriend and girlfriend?"

The question had come from so far out in left field that Luke couldn't think of a damned thing to say other than, "Is that what you want?"

"Well," Kolt said, hanging by his knees from the web's top rope strand. "You are, like, my mom and dad, which means you're s'posed to be married, so I guess it'd be okay, but it would be better for me if you were married, 'cause that way it'd be easier talking about you guys with kids from school. But then you guys fight a lot, so it's probably a bad idea."

Luke's chest tightened. It hadn't occurred to him that in this day and age kids even cared if parents were together or divorced or never married.

"Why haven't you talked about this before?"

Shrugging, Kolt admitted, "You never asked."

Marriage. Wow. Luke would be lying if he said he

hadn't thought about the notion—especially with Daisy. But that had been back in high school when his most important goals had been passing Chem II and finding something fun to do on any given Saturday night.

Since Daisy's revelation about Kolt, Luke would've expected his parents to press the wedding issue. Far from it, they'd urged him to keep things casual between him and Daisy.

Oddly enough, even Georgina, who was a renowned stickler for having all of her offspring wed the moment children became involved, hadn't said so much as a peep on the topic. At least not to Luke. Did she feel the same as Dallas when it came to the topic of a reunion?

If so, why did that make him feel about six inches tall?

Moreover, why did he care what Daisy's family thought of him? He never wanted her back, did he?

"I'M CURIOUS," LUKE SAID to Daisy after they'd both tucked Kolt into bed. They sat on the front porch, cloaked in darkness save for the flickering gaslights. The temperature was, for once, in the comfortable eighties, and crickets sang in conjunction with occasional house-rattling explosions coming from Dallas's movie room. "Why do you think your mom hasn't wanted us to marry?"

"E-excuse me?" Judging by her expression, Luke's question took Daisy by surprise.

"She practically held your brothers at gunpoint to marry Josie and Wren. Should my feelings be hurt she doesn't want me in the family?"

"Where is this coming from?" Daisy asked. "Days ago you confirmed you want nothing to do with me. Now, all of the sudden you want to talk marriage?"

"No. That's not at all what I said. What I want to know is, does Georgina think that the two of us would be a poor match? Dallas does. In fact, at the cookout, he pretty much warned me to steer clear of you."

"Why?" Daisy leaned forward sharply enough to set the frame of her chair creaking. "How is what we do even any of his business?"

"It's not," Luke said, "but I can see how Dallas would feel protective toward you. Especially with what went down with Henry right under his nose." When she failed to comment, he probed, "What are you thinking?"

Her eyes had turned glassy. Was she tearing? "God's honest truth, I love the idea of us being a family. An official family. But we both know there's more to it than that."

"You think?" He hoped his half smile sent the message he was teasing.

"You know what I mean. Loving the idea of something isn't enough to sustain a marriage for the next fifty years. Let's say we were to put aside our differences in order to stay together until Kolt leaves for college, then what? Would we still want to be with each other?" When he didn't answer, she noted, "Now you're the quiet one."

"Guess I have a lot on my mind."

"I'm sorry Kolt mentioned what his friends at school have been saying. While I hate his being given a hard time about anything, let alone an issue that's in our power to fix, that's not a good enough reason to marry. Agreed?"

Though Luke nodded, stress knotted the base of his neck. He didn't want to marry Daisy, but he resented like hell having first Dallas, then her tell him it would be a bad idea. He hadn't thought of it before, but aside from taking Daisy to court, marriage would be the most certain and relatively painless way to ensure Luke got to spend as much time as possible with his son. It was the perfect solution for all concerned parties.

Too bad from the sounds of it Daisy would never agree.

Chapter Thirteen

"You are so welcome," Daisy said to her client Jane Richmond, who'd just received her first child-support payment in over two years. After returning Jane's hug, Daisy walked her out of the office, closing the door behind her.

Moments like these made her glad she'd chosen this path.

As opposed to Sunday night's awkward conversation, during which she'd wished she could hide beneath her chair. Yes, she would like nothing more than for Luke and her to become an official family, but she wouldn't beg.

Back at her desk, she lost herself in a file Barb had sent. The case was a meaty corporate cover-up that took her mind off Luke.

At least until he walked in the door.

Dressed in jeans, a dirt-smudged white T-shirt, boots and what she knew to be his favorite cowboy hat, he looked good enough to kiss until she was too weak-kneed to stand. "Hey," he said with a tip of his stupid, sexy hat, "I'm not interrupting anything, am I?"

"Nope." *Yes.* She had at least another three hours before she should even think about taking a break. Too bad for her, Luke looked so damned gorgeous.

"In that case, how about taking a stroll? It's the kind of day Weed Gulch only sees a few times a year. Not too hot. Not too cold. No wind. No ragweed. I'm pretty sure it's a criminal offense not to be out there enjoying it."

His argument was ludicrous, but at the same time, sadly true. Laughing, she pushed back her chair. "Yes, Luke, I will stroll with you, but only if we head toward ice cream."

"Done." He crooked his arm, and she slipped hers through it.

Outside, Daisy tipped her face to the sun. "Wow. I'd forgotten how good it feels not to run from place to place in the eternal search for air conditioning."

"You really are something," Luke said.

She glanced his way to find him staring. "What did I do?"

"You're beautiful. After all this time, I still feel like a geeky freshman checking out the hottest cheerleader."

"Luke Montgomery," she chastised, "you were never a geek. More like a god."

"Your history's a bit skewed," he said with a devilish grin, "but you won't hear me complaining."

When Luke shockingly held out his hand for her to hold, Daisy eased her fingers between his. The simple touch hit her with an erotic jolt. Pulse racing, it was all she could do to keep from skipping like a giddy little girl.

They got ice cream—Luke chocolate and Daisy had a vanilla twist—and chose a picnic table well away from the others on the grassy lawn. Again Daisy was struck with the pleasant and rare sensation that nothing needed to be said. They'd known each other for so long that they knew each other's highlights. All they were missing were the gaps from the past ten years. Those could be filled in easily enough. Assuming Luke wanted them to be.

Finished with his cone, he wadded his napkin and tossed it basketball-style into a rusty trash barrel.

"Nice," she said when his shot made it in. "That was well within the three-point range."

"Thanks." He grinned at her before sharply looking away. "Look, I feel rotten about buying you ice cream under false pretenses."

"Oh?" Just when her heart had resumed its normal sedate pace, his new, pensive expression set her on edge.

"I need to apologize for Sunday, as I wasn't entirely honest with you."

"In what regard?" Daisy managed to ask even though she wasn't sure she wanted to know.

"When you made me agree that we have no business marrying, I meant it. But then I got to thinking…what if we did? But not for love or anything like that, but custody?"

"Please tell me you're kidding?"

His earnest expression said he was dead serious. "I'd be lying if I said I haven't toyed with the notion of having a lawyer write up something to bind Kolt to me legally, but this is even better. And cheaper."

"Are you insane?" She had never been more insulted. So much so that if they hadn't been in public she'd have pitched her ice cream at his ridiculously handsome face!

"AM I FORGIVEN?" LUKE ASKED when Daisy picked him up at his cabin to go on a combined trip to Tulsa. The first order of business on the crisp, second Saturday in October was selecting kitchen cabinets at a custom shop. Then they'd hit up a few Halloween specialty stores for costumes.

Kolt lightly snored in the backseat.

"The jury's still out," Daisy said. With her hair in a ponytail and face scrubbed clean of makeup, she looked even prettier than the last time he'd seen her.

"I'm sorry. In hindsight, I realize the whole marriage-for-custody thing wasn't one of my better ideas."

"You think?" Her glare confirmed his suspicions that it might be a long day. Kolt had been the one who'd invited him, and as he'd gradually warmed toward his father, no matter what Daisy thought, there was no way Luke was going turn his kid's invitation down.

"What's with the message on your back window?" he asked while climbing into the passenger seat. "'I See You' is written in the dust."

Shaking her head, she pointed to their sleeping child. "Kolt thinks it's hilarious how I never can get all of the dust off my car. Our budding artist enjoys drawing faces and messages in the dirt."

"He shows promise," Luke teased, hoping to lighten the mood.

"I'd rather he became familiar with a soapy rag and bucket."

Fastening his seat belt, Luke leaned his head back, settling in for what he guessed would be a not-so-entertaining day.

"I WANNA BE A SLASHER, chainsaw-killer guy," Kolt announced at Ehrle's. Though it wasn't the biggest costume store in Tulsa, Daisy remembered shopping there with her dad and brothers when she was a little girl.

"Sweetie," Daisy said, trying to keep her calm while a cajillion other kids darted down the aisle. "You're a little young for that degree of violence. How do you even know what that is?"

Raising his chin, he said, "We watch slasher movies with Jonah's big brother. They're cool. I'm gonna carry Uncle Dallas's chainsaw, too."

"No, you're not," Daisy said.

"Why not? Everyone else is."

Daisy tried counting to ten in her head, but only made it to three. "What have I told you about that argument not holding up in court?"

"That it won't?" Kolt rolled his eyes.

Stopping on the monster aisle, Luke said to their son, "If I were you, I'd consider going with a Frankenstein theme. Not only do you get to paint yourself green, but you wear ripped clothes, have bolts sticking out of your forehead and carry a big club you can use to hit your friends."

"Cool!" All smiles, Kolt soon had everything he needed to become a classic monster. More importantly, in Daisy's mind, he'd gained yet one more reason to grow closer to his father.

THE NEXT SATURDAY, rain fell in gust-driven sheets, making for the perfect movie day. Luke had originally invited Kolt, but they'd voted that if Daisy didn't nag about eating healthy food, she could join them. She'd held up her end of the deal by fixing cheese dip and pizza rolls. Luke had already laid out a full supply of candy: Twizzlers and M&M's and Milk Duds.

"This is nice," Daisy said, curled under a blanket into the far corner of the sofa. "I can't remember the last time I've lounged an entire day."

"Me, neither."

Midway through *Jaws,* Kolt fell asleep in Luke's armchair. Something about seeing his son in his favorite chair felt deeply satisfying, as if a part of Luke had been filled that he hadn't even realized was empty. If only he could figure out how to manage his growing feelings for Daisy.

"Mom told me there's a Halloween dance at the Grange," Daisy mentioned, out of the blue. "I thought it might be fun. Would you want to go—strictly as friends?"

"Depends. What do you have in mind for costumes?" Was it wrong that Luke found her invitation flattering?

"I don't know. I haven't thought it out that far." Nibbling on a licorice stick, she suggested, "What about Han Solo and Chewbacca? Anthony and Cleopatra."

He blanched. "I'm not wearing a skirt."

"You be a martini and I'll be an olive."

"Cute, but logistically tough." Luke tried, "Angel and Devil?"

"Who gets to be the angel?"

"Me," Luke said without a hitch.

Now Daisy was making faces.

"Got it," he said. "I'll be a creepy ghost and you, a sexy ghost buster."

"Loving this." He loved the way her whole face glowed when she was excited.

"YOU'RE AWFULLY SMILEY TODAY." Georgina was making good on her promise to tame the gardens in front of Daisy and Kolt's new home. They'd already cleared a small forest of brush and weeds and had just unearthed a stone-walled flowerbed complete with a few barely surviving rosebushes.

"I'm happy," Daisy admitted. "For the first time in a long while, I feel on top of the world."

Sitting on her gardening stool, Georgina said, "You can't imagine how good that makes me feel—especially when I've worried about you for so long."

Eyes stinging, Daisy asked, "Can you ever forgive me?"

"Already done."

The weather was beyond idyllic—the temperature in the low eighties with high, puffy clouds and not a breath of wind. The summer had been long and mercilessly hot.

It felt as if the whole world now sighed in relief. Daisy included.

After weeding awhile in companionable silence, Georgina said, "Josie and I have noticed you and Luke spending a lot of time together. Anything juicy to report?"

Where to start? "I invited him to the Grange Halloween dance and he accepted."

"That's a step in the right direction. Is this an outing with Kolt, or for grown-ups only?"

"If I ask you to babysit, does that give you a clue?"

Georgina laughed. "You know I'm always pleased as punch to watch Kolt. What costumes are you two wearing?"

Daisy outlined their plans, asking her mom to save a few cans for her to paint and then transform into toolbelt gadgets.

"Is Luke going to be a white-sheet ghost or a more original variety?"

"We're thinking of going with makeup and dirt-smudged clothes."

Laughing, Georgina said, "Sounds like you'll make a lovely—albeit, smelly—couple."

Growing misty, Daisy admitted, "I don't know if that's what we officially are, but I'd like to be."

"Give it time." Tugging extra hard on a clump of crabgrass, Georgina grunted. "You young people are too impatient. Let the boy woo you."

"Mom, I've waited ten years to return to Luke, which is why I finally decided to woo him. I'm tired of waiting."

"Then why didn't you come home sooner?"

"Wish I had an answer." There it was again—at the crux of Daisy's every issue was the worst act she'd ever committed. For so many years she'd harbored guilt over what had happened with Henry. She'd needlessly, stupidly blamed herself when, as a child, she'd been cruelly victimized. How much longer would fate keep punishing her? More than anything, she longed for a fresh start, but the questions kept coming, dragging her to an emotional void where she no longer wanted to be.

"DAMN, YOU LOOK HOT," LUKE SAID, standing at the Buckhorn Ranch front door to be greeted by the sexiest damn ghost hunter he'd ever seen. Daisy had only been able to find men's coveralls, so she'd borrowed her mother's sewing machine to produce a custom fit. Either she was crazy talented to have cut them to hug her every curve, or she'd gotten scissor-happy. Regardless, the view made him the winner.

"Looking good is my secret ghost-busting technique. I lure you in before sucking you into my ghost trap." She tapped one of the multitude of silver canisters dangling from her tool belt.

"If it's that much fun being caught, why would I want to do any more roaming?" Though he'd meant the statement to be a joke, Luke realized the more he was with Daisy, the more she felt like an addiction. But in a good way.

"Excellent answer," she said with a heady smile. "Ready to go?"

"Let me say a quick hi to Kolt."

"He's in Dallas's theater room. That thing is obscene." Daisy led the way. Her costume looked equally great from behind.

"Obscenely fabulous," Luke noted.

She shot him an over-the-shoulder dirty look.

"Boo!" Luke sneaked up behind his son, making his best scary face.

Kolt jumped a good foot out of his plush movie chair.

"Luke, you scared me half to death! Your costume's awesome!"

Kolt's friend, Jonah, popped out of the chair beside him. "Whoa! You're the coolest dad ever!"

While Dallas paused *The Haunted Mansion* and flipped on the lights, Bonnie and Betsy and Josie also admired Luke's costume.

"You're so lucky," Jonah said to Kolt. "My parents never do anything this cool."

"Yeah," Kolt said, ambushing Luke with a monster-size hug. "I like my mom and dad a whole lot."

"YOU'RE AWFULLY QUIET," Daisy said to Luke halfway to the Grange hall.

"To tell you the truth," he said, tightening his grip on the wheel. "I'm having a tough time keeping it together. Kolt's hug was epic."

"There's plenty more where that came from," she said with an impromptu squeeze to his right hand.

"I can't wait. It's funny, but I can't remember life without him. In such a short time, Kolt has come to mean everything to me."

"I'm glad—for both of you." Luke's words served as a powerful aphrodisiac. Daisy had never adored him more.

By the time they reached the party, it was already in full swing. There were witches and a Dolly Parton and a giant purple crayon. Meeting up with many of their old high-school friends was fun, but also hard. Daisy lost count of the number of times she was asked where she'd been. An equally hot topic was how she was coping with being back in the same town as Henry. Honestly, what made people think she'd want to discuss something like that on a night designated for fun?

"Daisy!" her old chemistry lab partner, Tammy, squealed. She'd squeezed into her cheerleading uniform and her husband, Blake, wore his Weed Gulch football jersey. "Oh, my God, when we heard about what y'all's ranch foreman did to you, we were amazed Dallas hadn't shot him dead. How in the world are you coping?"

Daisy reached for Luke's hand, his support. "It's been tough, but I'm getting by."

"I was so tickled to hear y'all are finally getting married. My mom says you're having another baby and that's why you bought the old Peterson place."

Wow. Daisy wasn't sure where to start on damage control.

"Your mom must really get around," Luke said with his most charming smile over blaring country music. "Daisy and I didn't even know we were having another baby, let alone getting married." He winked. "We did know she bought a house, though. It kind of matches my costume."

After taking a moment to process his dig, Tammy's smile faded. "You don't have to be rude, Luke Montgomery."

"But I'm so glad he was." Daisy stood on her tiptoes to give her favorite ghost a kiss on his cheek.

While their old friend flounced off, Luke asked, "Want to get the hell out of here?"

"Thought you'd never ask."

They were quiet all the way to Luke's cabin. It was chilly, so Luke started a fire.

Daisy scrounged in his kitchen for a bottle of wine.

"That's better," he said after scrubbing off his white face paint and sitting next to Daisy on the sofa. "Want music?"

She shook her head. "I like the fire's crackle."

"I can't stop myself from liking you." They kissed, drank wine, kissed more until Daisy felt as loose and hot as the flames. How many years had she longed for just this, and now it felt as if her every dream were on the verge of coming true.

"Does the small-town gossip bother you?" Luke asked, skimming her palms with his thumbs, in the process shooting pleasurable tingles through her body.

"Not as much as what you're doing."

"I'm serious." He stopped to cup her face, directing her focus on him. "Tammy's own personal rumor mill had to sting. How are you coping?"

Daisy shrugged. Some days were better than others. "Aside from keeping Kolt from you, I've done nothing to be ashamed of."

"Day by day, I'm learning to deal," he said, nuzzling her neck. "Time for you to forgive yourself."

His words acted as a balm to her soul. Ten seemingly endless years she'd harbored such guilt and fear. To even think of letting it go filled her with such relief she wasn't sure how to handle the overflow of emotion.

"I—I want to be with you," she said, pressing her hand to his dear cheek. No matter what she'd told herself, she'd always wanted to be with him.

"You are." He bowed his head to nuzzle her throat.

"Men…" Since he didn't get her hint, she gave him a bonus clue and eased her hands under his T-shirt to drag it over his head. Pressing her lips to the warm skin of his pecs, she said, "How's a girl supposed to get any action when her guy's so dense?"

"*Oooh.*" His grin fluttered her pulse. "Why didn't you say so?"

"I thought I had." Unbuttoning her jumpsuit, she wriggled her shoulders free.

"Damn," he whispered, "you're stunning."

"You're not too bad yourself." Skimming her hands along his chest and over his shoulders, she explored him anew, as if he were a beloved, tranquil glade where she'd always found the freedom to escape her everyday life.

"You and our son," Luke said, voice thick with emotion, "mean the world to me."

"We feel the same about you."

Taking their time, they made a game of shedding each other's clothes. Luke's pants. Daisy's bra. Layer by layer, they stripped not only the physical items keeping them apart, but any last emotional holds.

As they laughed and caressed and tickled each other onto the soft rug in front of the fire, their kissing lost its playful edge, taking on the urgency of two people who had been apart too long.

When Luke entered her, Daisy sucked in her breath. It had been so long. A moment's pain eased into budding pleasure until she lost the ability to think. Every nerve in her body became attuned to his. Arching up, she pressed her fingers into his smooth back, willing him deeper.

"I love you," she said at the crest of her pleasure.

He tensed, driving into her one last shuddering time.

Had he even heard her? Or did he not feel the same? How was she supposed to know?

"Lord, I've missed you," he said, rolling aside only to cradle her close. He skimmed his fingers over her hair, kissed her closed eyelids and the tip of her nose. When she began crying, he kissed away her tears. "What's wrong?"

"Nothing." *Everything!* She'd told him she loved him and he hadn't so much as acknowledged her words. Hardly an expert on relationships, she didn't know whether to call him on it, or let it be.

"Then why the tears? I didn't hurt you, did I?"

Not in the way you think. "No. It was beautiful. But it's late, and I should probably get back to Kolt."

"Are you sure?" In the fire's glow, he searched her expression. No doubt seeking clues as to what had brought on her change in mood. But she wasn't giving any. When it came to putting her heart on the line, she'd gone as far as she was willing to go. No matter what, she knew she'd always love him, but she deserved for him to love her, too.

Wearing nothing but unfastened jeans, Luke walked her to his Jeep, wincing when the gravel bit his bare feet. "Guess I might've wanted to put more clothes, on, huh?"

"At least shoes," she snapped.

"All right," he said, pinning her to the vehicle's grill by bracing his hands on either side of her. "Out with it. What did I do to tick you off?"

"I told you I love you and you ignored me. I have a right to be upset."

He rocked back to ease his fingers into his hair. "I heard you. I wanted to tell you I love you, but I still— hell, what you put me through isn't easy to let go. Give me time, all right?" Cradling her tearstained cheek, he said, "I can't make promises, but for once in a long time, we're on the right track."

"Great," she said with a sniffle. "Just what every girl longs to hear."

"You're not a girl," he reminded, "but a full-grown woman who damn near emotionally killed me. How do I know you won't do it again?"

"Trick or Treat!" Kolt and Jonah shouted at the door of a white bungalow in one of the town's oldest neighborhoods.

Daisy stood with Luke at the end of the driveway, shivering despite their many layers of clothing. Forecasters predicted one of the earliest snows they'd seen in years. Teeth chattering, she said, "Welcome to Oklahoma, huh? One month you're so hot you feel like you're melting and the next, you think your hair's frozen."

If only the night they'd made love had ended differently, tonight could have been romantic and silly and fun. As it was, Daisy was suffering through it merely for the sake of their son.

In a perfect world, she'd have warded off another fit of shivers by slipping her arms around Luke's waist. Instead, she hugged herself.

By the time they'd followed Kolt and Jonah five more homes down the block, snow was falling. Big, gumball-size flakes that melted on the road, but stuck to lawns, tree limbs and cars.

Ten houses later, Luke said, "It's damn cold. Couldn't we run the kids by Reasor's and let them pick whatever candy they want?"

"Works for me," Daisy said, no longer able to keep her teeth from chattering.

Luke told the bundled-up boys they were calling it quits, and though they weren't happy, they began the long return trip to the car with a minimum of whining, instead, running ahead, staging an epic snow battle with Kolt's Frankenstein club and Jonah's pirate sword.

At Luke's Jeep, Daisy was surprised to find the words, I See You written in the snow on the back window. "Is that for me or your dad?" Daisy asked Kolt.

"Huh?" He was so busy walloping Jonah with his club, he hadn't heard her question. Daisy pointed to the car. "Didn't you write that?"

"No," he said. "Am I in trouble?"

She shook her head. "You did write it on my car those other two times though, right?"

Hopping on the curb, he said, "I don't know what you're talking about and I really have to pee."

"Me, too," Jonah said.

"Climb in, guys." Luke had clicked the remote key button, unlocking the doors.

Inside, with the heater blasting not very warm air, Daisy felt as if she could've stood before a raging fire and still been chilled to her core. With the boys chatting in the back, she asked Luke, "If Kolt hasn't been writing that message on my car and now yours, then who? Would Henry be that brazen?"

"It's possible," Luke said, making a right. "But why? He's no dummy. Surely he realizes that if he so much as looks cockeyed at you, you'll press charges. Maybe it was Betsy or Bonnie?"

"But they aren't with us tonight."

"True."

Hands over her face, she said, "I don't know what I'd do if this all started up again. I really don't."

"Relax," he urged, rubbing her forearm. "This is probably a fluke coincidence. Trust me, everything's going to be fine."

A WEEK LATER, LYING ON A BLANKET beneath the big oak in his parents' backyard, Luke was grateful for the sun's return. What he wasn't thrilled about was the way two of his favorite people were so incompatible.

His mother, still trying to make up for lost time with Kolt, was hosting yet another party. This time, a

Saturday-afternoon fiesta. Odd, considering there were only a few weeks until Thanksgiving, but he'd long since learned, when it came to his mother and parties, to stay out of her way.

Too bad he'd forgotten to give Daisy the memo.

"Daisy," his mother said, "while I appreciate you trying to help, I wanted the napkins fanned on the drink table."

"I thought they might get wet from spilled ice over there, which is why I put them alongside the plates. Makes for a better traffic flow."

Oh, boy...

On his feet, Luke hustled to get between them before either woman threw the first punch. "I think those napkins would look amazing right here," he said, taking the pile and setting them alongside the forks. "What do you think, Kolt?"

The boy glanced up from his game to scrunch his nose. "Is it time to eat?"

"There you have it." Luke put his arms around both women. "The deciding vote. I knew Kolt would side with me."

While his mother glared, Daisy couldn't hide her smile.

An hour later, the gathering was in full swing with all of the cousins and aunts and uncles cramming their pie holes with Mexican food. His family loved to eat—any occasion would do.

Luke took extra care to reintroduce Daisy to everyone and if they launched personal questions, he cut them off midstream. He cared for Daisy—deeply. While he might not be ready to say the words of commitment she longed to hear, no way would he let anyone hurt her again.

"Aren't you the little gal who just bought the old Peterson place?" Uncle Frank held a taquito in one hand and a whiskey sour in his other.

"Yes, sir, I am," Daisy said. She sipped at her tall-neck Corona.

"Back in the day, that old house was really something. Every bit as fine as your daddy's ranch, but in a different way. Real hoity-toity fancy. You just holler if you need help."

"Thank you. I appreciate your offer, and will put you at the top of my guest list for my first party."

"I'd appreciate it. So would the wife."

With his uncle ambling back to the buffet table, Luke leaned in close to Daisy, "See? My family isn't all bad."

"Did I ever say they *all* were?"

"Not in so many words," he admitted, "but it seems to me you left pretty early the last time Mom hosted one of her get-togethers."

"Can you blame me? Everyone acted as if Kolt was an angel, and I was just the evil witch who'd brought him into the world."

Luke couldn't help but burst out laughing. "I think you're exaggerating a wee bit."

"I'd say let's grab Kolt and ask his opinion, but considering how many presents he got that day, I doubt he'll be on my side."

Taking Daisy's hand and leading her into the quiet

spot between the overgrown lilac and the azaleas, Luke stole a few kisses.

"Stop," Daisy said, hands against his chest. "We're going to get caught and then your mom's going to call my mom and accuse me of public indecency in her backyard."

"Would that be so bad?" Luke asked, unbuttoning the top of her blouse.

"Stop!" she cried in a whispered shriek. "Do you want your mother thinking I'm a cheap floozy?"

"I don't care what she thinks," he confessed. "But *your* opinion means the world."

Her expression softened. "All right, that was sweet enough to get you temporarily out of the doghouse, but I still refuse to stand here making out."

"Then what are we going to do, because honestly, this party is boring as hell."

"For starters, we should find Kolt. Last I saw him, he'd eaten enough bean dip to explode."

Luke winced. "That could be ugly. Now I'm really glad he's bunking with you."

Daisy elbowed Luke hard to his ribs.

They searched the crowd of about twenty gathered in the backyard and another ten inside. They checked all of his family's bedrooms and the den and even the front yard and garage. Worse yet, everyone they asked remembered recently seeing him, but didn't know where he'd gone.

"Where could he be?" Daisy asked. She stood in the center of the quiet road.

"Beats the heck out of me. It's not like him to run

off." There were only six homes on the street. One by one, they asked neighbors who weren't at the party if they'd seen Kolt. None had.

"Luke, I'm scared." Daisy gripped his hand for all she was worth. "You don't think Henry had something to do with this, do you?"

"No way. Come on." Luke led her back to his parents' house. "As late as he's been staying up with Jonah, he's probably conked out in a quiet corner, snoring."

They searched the house again, but still came up with no Kolt. Luke hated alerting his mother, but it looked like they needed help.

Upon making an announcement that Kolt was missing, all present shot into action, not only canvassing the neighborhood, but climbing into cars and searching nearby streets as well.

Daisy went outside to see if by some off chance Kolt had fallen asleep in her car.

When Luke heard her scream, he bolted out after her.

"Look!" she cried, pointing at the back window of her car. In the dust someone had written:

I See You, but I'd Rather See Kolt.

Chapter Fourteen

"I'm gonna get in a lot of trouble if I don't tell my mom where I am," Kolt said to Henry who'd told him Uncle Cash's baby was hurt. "Why didn't you ask my mom or Luke to help Robin?"

"In times like this," Henry said, "babies like kids best. I'm sure your mom would agree. Besides, I looked everywhere and couldn't find your parents. Your uncle said to bring you right away. I'm good friends with him."

"Oh." The farther they got from his grandparents' house, the more worried Kolt became. In San Francisco, his teachers had talked lots about Stranger Danger, but there weren't any homeless people or weirdos in Weed Gulch. Everyone he'd met was nice. And anyway, no matter what his mom said, Henry wasn't a stranger and he'd always been nice to him.

"I thought we were going to Uncle Cash's house?" Kolt asked.

"We are," Henry promised. "We'll need to make a quick stop at my house first. I have lots of medicine."

"Are you a doctor and a ranch guy?" Kolt asked.

"Sort of. I make children feel *really* good." He smiled. "Hungry? There's lots of candy in there." Pointing to a cool Spiderman lunch-box, he said, "You know, with baby Robin's emergency and all, I forgot to tell you how glad I am that we're getting to hang out again. I have a feeling we're going to be special friends."

PANICKED DIDN'T BEGIN to describe Daisy's state of mind. Immediately upon finding the message on her car, Luke had called the sheriff and Daisy's mother, who were on their way to Luke's parents' house.

Dallas knew people who'd reportedly seen Henry coming and going from a few different places. The town's small police force had been dispatched to most. Luke, Dallas, Cash and Wyatt were checking the rest.

Daisy wanted to help in the search, but as distraught as she was, Luke had urged her to stay with his family.

Finally, Georgina arrived and Daisy ran into her mother's arms. "So help me, Mom, if that crazy old monster hurts our son, I don't know what I'll do."

"Kolt's a smart boy. He's not going to take any funny business without putting up a mighty fight."

Drawing back, horrified, Daisy asked, "What does that mean? Are you implying that because of what I *let* happen to me, I wasn't smart?"

"Don't go putting words in my mouth. That's not at all what I said. I meant you've raised a savvy young man who knows how to protect himself."

"Don't you get it?" Daisy asked. "*I* was savvy and knew how to protect myself, but that didn't help me.

What Henry did inherently changed me. Made me feel dirty and bad. I don't want my son bearing that kind of shame. I should've never come back here. Never."

Luke's mom marched across the room. "You dare take my grandson so much as one foot over the county line and I'll have you arrested. Haven't you already hurt my son enough? Luke's a wonderful man. All I've ever wanted was for him to get you once and for all out of his mind. Daisy Buckhorn, you're like a poison. As much as I love Kolt, I wish we could keep him and get rid of you. That way, Henry Pohl would never have touched our lives."

The pain in Daisy's chest hurt worse than any heart attack. It was a squeezing, vicelike torture that made her want to lash out and slap the woman across her condemning face.

"Peggy Montgomery," Georgina said, hands on her hips, eyes sparking, "since you stole my lunch back in sixth grade, I never have liked you. You're a bitter old woman who still isn't over losing the Prom Queen title to me."

"Stop," Daisy begged, stepping between the two bickering women. "Mrs. Montgomery, I couldn't care less what you think of me, but my son—your grandson—is out there somewhere, possibly hurt. Do you mind putting aside your own agenda long enough for us to get Kolt home safely?"

"THIS POP TASTES KINDA FUNNY," Kolt said. The house where his old friend, Henry, had taken him was kinda scary. It smelled like pee and was dark inside. The only place to sit was on a sofa that had holes in the cushions.

"It's a new flavor. You know how companies are always switching up their recipes to make you think it's a new product when in reality, all they want is more money."

"Um, yeah," Kolt said, taking another drink. "I'm feeling sleepy. Are we going to go help my baby cousin soon?"

"Very soon. I have a few more things to finish up here—you know, collecting my tools and such. Then, we'll be all ready to go."

Kolt was so sleepy, he could hardly understand what Henry was talking about.

"That's right," Henry said, sitting next to him on the couch. "Close your pretty eyes and your new best friend will make all your dreams come true."

"THIS IS BS," LUKE SAID, slamming the heel of his hand against the steering wheel. "Where could that sleazebag be?" He and Dallas had followed the directions they'd been given with no results. The road had diminished to little more than a four-wheel-drive path leading through dense forest.

"Keep going," Dallas urged. "I swear Wyatt and I came hunting out here once. Seems like there's a shack where this dead-ends."

"If we do find him, Dallas, and he has my son, you're going to have to hold me back to keep me from killing him."

With his fist, Dallas smacked his open palm. "Not if

I get to him first. Then you'll be the one needing to hold me. Way I see it, though, we both need to be smart. No sense in us going to jail for hurting Henry. That would only cause more grief for our families."

"My head gets that point, but every other piece of me wants to beat Henry to a bloody pulp."

Dallas nodded. "No one wants to pulverize this guy more than me. We'll have to work together to keep our cool—if he's even here."

Cresting the next hill, Luke saw a structure built of plywood and corrugated metal. What looked to be aluminum trailer windows had been fitted to the side. Seeing no vehicle made the pain in his already tight neck burn.

"Dammit," Dallas said. "I thought for sure he'd be here. It was the most isolated spot anywhere on our list."

"Wait," Luke said, "what's that?"

Only the corner of a chrome truck fender was visible beneath a camouflage tarp further disguised with pine boughs and twigs.

"Let's check it out. Cut the engine here." A good two hundred yards from the shack, Luke killed the motor, then together they crept to the truck, tossing back the wrap to find it was indeed Henry's.

Adrenaline surged through Luke, along with the hope that he'd find Kolt safe inside.

"Come on," Dallas said, "I'll cover the back, you get the front. We both have a score to settle with this bastard, but your son's safety trumps all."

"Agreed."

Not in the mood for pleasantries, Luke tried the door and found it locked, then kicked the flimsy barrier down.

Lying inordinately still on a beat-up sofa was his son, Henry hovering protectively over him—holding a knife to his throat. "Go ahead," Henry taunted. "Step one foot closer and I'll gut him like a hog."

"Back off," Luke said. "You're in enough trouble as it is. Let Kolt go and I'll bet any judge will take it easy on you."

"Let him go?" Henry laughed. "After what his bitch mother said I did? She ruined my reputation. My whole life. I can't go anywhere without so-called friends accusing me of horrible things. All I ever did was love the children of this town. Is it really my fault if so many of them have loved me back?"

Luke's stomach turned at the implication that Daisy wasn't Henry's only victim.

"Dad?" Kolt sluggishly turned his head. His movements were exaggerated to the point that it didn't take a rocket scientist to figure out he'd been drugged. "Dad, is that you?"

While Luke's knees felt rubbery with relief, he knew they weren't anywhere out of the woods just yet.

"Good," Henry said, "my new friend's awake. Before you so rudely interrupted, Luke, I'd planned some nap-time fun, but it's just as easy to play while Kolt's alert."

Luke clenched his hands so tightly his fingernails cut into his palms. More than anything he wanted to jump

Henry and take him down, but as long as he held the knife to Kolt's jugular, Luke had to play it safe.

From the corner of his eye, Luke caught a movement and realized Dallas was stepping up behind Henry, biding his time until he felt it safe to make a move.

Dallas held his finger to his lips.

Luke barely nodded.

Henry brushed Kolt's hair back from his forehead. "You're so handsome. I've always preferred to play with little girls, but considering how much you remind me of your mother, you'll do."

With a mighty growl, Dallas lunged for Henry, pinning the arm holding the knife.

Luke then took down the rest of him, with one mighty punch rendering Henry unconscious. "Sorry," Luke said. "Self-defense."

Dallas said, "Couldn't agree more."

From outside came a siren's wail.

"While you were in here, I called for backup. Lucky for us, a few search teams weren't too far away."

"Dad?" Kolt tried sitting up, only to fall back down. "I feel funny."

Chills gripped Luke with such force he had to sit. Scooping his boy into his arms, Luke held him and rocked him and cried silent tears of relief. Not only had Kolt called him Dad, but the boy was going to be okay. He hadn't been physically hurt, and likely, once Henry's drug of choice wore off, Kolt would remember little of his ordeal.

As Henry began to stir, Dallas said to Luke, "Get Kolt out of here. I'll stand watch till help comes."

On his feet, Kolt in his arms, Luke noted red and blue lights strobing through the dirty windows onto the walls. "Lucky for that scumbag," he said with a nod toward Henry, "you won't have to wait too long."

UNABLE TO COPE WITH both her fears for her son and Peggy Montgomery's blame, Daisy had asked her mother to take her back to the ranch, where at least she could concentrate on Kolt.

"Honey," Georgina said, an hour into their wait, "you're going to wear a hole in the carpet. Sit down. Rest. You know Luke and Dallas will bring Kolt home."

"That's just it, Mom, even if Kolt is healthy and emotionally unscarred, how do we ever feel safe in this town again? Kolt was snatched right out from under us at a family party. It's insane."

"Yes, it is," Georgina said, rising to give Daisy a hug, "which is why you never need worry about an event like this happening again."

Shrugging free of Georgina's hold, Daisy continued to pace.

Fearing what Luke and Dallas might find, Josie had taken the twins and her baby to Wren's. That's how serious the situation was. No one wanted the girls overhearing details if their cousin had been killed.

Just as Daisy was contemplating this and continuing her pacing, the front door opened and in walked Dallas, followed by Luke, Kolt limp in his arms.

"Oh!" Daisy cried, running to be with her boys. "Is he all right? Did Henry—?"

"No. He's been drugged, but the effects wore off a while back. Now, I think he's just exhausted."

Luke carried Kolt to the couch. Daisy sat beside him, cradling his head to her breasts. "My sweet baby boy. I'm so sorry."

"Mommy," Kolt said. He hadn't called her that in a good four years. "Henry said he was my friend. He told me Uncle Cash needed my help with Robin and it was an emergency. I told him you'd be mad at me for leaving without telling you, but he said you'd understand and not be mad. Are you mad?"

"No, baby," Daisy managed past the knot in her throat, "I'm not mad at all."

"Henry wasn't really my friend, was he?"

Daisy shook her head, unable to speak through her tears.

WITH KOLT SCRUBBED head-to-toe clean and tucked into bed, Daisy refusing to leave his side, Luke headed to the kitchen for coffee and one of the sandwiches a neighbor had dropped off.

The sheriff had stopped by to report that with Kolt's testimony as well as that of a few other girls who had recently come forward, Henry would be locked away for a very long time.

Though the day had had a happy ending, Luke couldn't help but let his mind wander to dark places. What if Kolt had been seriously hurt? Worse yet, killed? How would he have held it together well enough to help Daisy through?

While they'd made love, Daisy had told Luke she

loved him. Luke hated himself for having pretended not to hear, but at the time he hadn't been entirely sure what love even meant. After the events of this afternoon, after nearly losing his boy, Luke now recognized that love was the yawning black hole in your gut that loomed when you got a glimpse of your life without the people you most adored.

"You all right?" Dallas asked, sauntering into the kitchen to pour himself a cup of coffee.

"Yeah." Grinning, Luke said, "oddly enough, I'm feeling pretty good. Sometime during all of this mess, I finally pulled my head out of my behind long enough to realize I'm crazy in love with your sister."

"About damned time," Dallas said with a pat to Luke's back.

"Since you're the man of the Buckhorn family, do I have your permission to ask her to marry me?"

Dallas laughed. "I'd have to go old-school, challenging you to a duel if you didn't."

"Thanks, man."

"My pleasure," Dallas said. "Welcome to the family."

The two lifelong friends hugged before Luke headed up the back stairs two at a time.

A KNOCK SOUNDED ON Kolt's open door.

Daisy looked up to see Luke. He'd never looked more handsome. His jeans might be torn and dirty, his once nice red plaid Western shirt crumpled and stained with what she'd learned was Henry's blood, but for saving their son, she'd forever be in Luke's debt.

"May I come in?" he asked.

"Of course." She'd stretched out beside Kolt on his twin bed.

Luke perched on what little extra room was left at the foot. "It's been a helluva day, huh?"

"That it has. Did you ever get around to calling your parents to let them know Kolt's okay?"

"A while ago," he said. "Mom wanted to come over, but thank goodness, Dad talked her out of it."

"Which reminds me," Daisy said, easing to her feet. While Kolt lightly snored, she gestured for Luke to follow her out of his room. "Your mom and I got into it after you left. She said incredibly hurtful things and I need to know if you agree."

"What kinds of things?" he asked in Daisy's room.

"That your whole family views me as a poison to you. That if it hadn't been for my influence in your life, you'd now be married and happy with six kids and a perfect house and—"

"Stop," he said, pulling her back when she tried escaping his embrace. "Not a single word of that is true. You and Kolt have come to mean everything to me. My intention in even being with you right now was to ask you to marry me, but the mood is kind of broken."

"What?" She looked up at him with huge, tear-stained doe eyes. Why, when she'd first left all those years ago, hadn't he moved heaven and earth to find her? How had he breathed with her gone? "Do you mean it? You really want to marry me?"

"Um, yeah."

Her smile rocked his world.

"Mom, GIVE IT A REST," Luke warned after Wednesday night's supper. She'd wanted Kolt to come, but Daisy still felt uncomfortable letting him out of her sight and she sure wanted nothing to do with Peggy and her big mouth. Besides which, Luke needed to have this conversation in private. "I'm marrying Daisy and that's that. If you don't like my choice in brides, feel free to skip our wedding."

"Son," his dad warned. "Don't you sass your mom. She means well."

"Bull," Luke grumbled. "What she means is to stick her gossipy nose where it doesn't belong."

"That's enough." Joe slapped his napkin on the dining-room table. "I will not have you talking to your mother like that in our home."

"Do you know what she said to Daisy? She had the gall to call her a poison in my life. Did Mom confess to that?"

"I was standing beside her when she said it," his dad admitted, "but in her defense, you're not being logical where Daisy or your son is concerned. Daisy ran off once, hid Kolt from you for practically his whole life. What's to say she won't try it again? Right in our living room she declared in front of God and everyone that she wished she'd never returned to Weed Gulch. If she took off again with Kolt, running to Lord only knows where, what would you do? There's nothing on paper anywhere to prove you're Kolt's father. You'd have to track down your son, force DNA tests, get hung up in court. It's bound to be a big old donkey mess." Pushing his chair back from the table, Joe rose to stare at the family portrait they'd had taken a good twenty years earlier. "Son, I know you love this woman, but what do you really know about her? All your mother and I are asking is that you take a few legal precautions before getting into a mess you can't fight your way out of. After all, she is a lawyer, and you know how wily they can be."

His entire life, Luke had looked up to his parents. He'd admired their lifestyle and sought them out for advice. On this matter, however, they were completely at odds.

"I'm sorry you feel this way," Luke said, tossing his own napkin on the table. "Guess I'd better get going."

"Thank your mother for dinner. She worked on it all afternoon."

Ever the dutiful son, Luke did as his father requested on that one issue. As for the matter of marrying Daisy, his family needed to back off.

He didn't have a clue what his legal rights were regarding Kolt, and considering how Luke felt about Daisy, he didn't much care. Once they were married, and Kolt shared Luke's last name, the whole world would know him as Luke's son. That fact meant more than any legal document.

Luke wished he could believe that.

Chapter Fifteen

Saturday night, after having worked on her house all day, Daisy was excited about her date with Luke. It was almost Thanksgiving and this year, she had an extraordinary amount of blessings for which to be thankful.

Henry had been denied bail and was most likely behind bars for good. Kolt was back at school, unscarred by his ordeal. The psychiatrist she and Luke had taken him to reported that Kolt was actually lucky to have been drugged as it had saved him the trauma of realizing he'd been kidnapped, rather than enlisted to save his cousin. Best of all, she and Luke had decided to follow in Cash's footsteps by having a Christmas wedding. To say Georgina was thrilled was the understatement of the year. From the moment she'd heard the news, the woman had started planning.

Dressing in her best black dress, then adding her favorite pearls, Daisy realized the only dim spot in her otherwise bright life was Peggy Montgomery. They hadn't spoken since the afternoon Kolt had been taken. Daisy knew she couldn't put off seeing the woman forever, but she figured a year or two wouldn't be so bad.

"Where are we going?" Daisy asked in the Jeep once they were finally underway.

"Wouldn't you like to know," he teased.

"Yes." She unbuckled her seat belt to string kisses round his neck. "I would."

"Hey," he complained. "Buckle up for safety."

"You're no fun."

"Oh," Luke laughed, "wait about five minutes and you'll be eating those words."

No kidding.

He pulled into the driveway of her new home, only, instead of being dark and dreary as it had been when she'd left, white Christmas lights had been strung from the turrets and cupolas and eaves.

"Luke, it's amazing." She bounded out of the car for a better view. "But when… I was here all afternoon."

Standing next to her, his arm around her waist, he said, "You forget you have three brothers who have an awful lot of friends. Ever heard the expression, 'Many hands make light work'? The second you drove off, they swooped in."

Beaming, she shook her head. "This is incredible. I don't know how to thank you."

"How about by wearing this?" From his coat pocket, in night air cold enough that they could see their breath, he withdrew a robin's-egg-blue box.

"You remembered?" When they'd been teens, she'd been obsessed with the movie, *Breakfast at Tiffany's,* and had once told Luke if a man didn't buy her a ring from there, she'd refuse to marry him.

He nodded. "In the movie, I know Audrey Hepburn

really gets a Cracker Jack ring, but they don't put rings in Cracker Jack anymore, so you'll have to settle for the real thing."

Tearing up, she stood on her tiptoes, kissing him for all she was worth. "It's the most gorgeous ring in the whole world."

"For what it cost, it'd better be," he said with a wink.

She kissed him again.

"Let's get inside before we freeze."

"But the central heat won't be done for two more weeks."

Taking her hand, Luke explained, "That's why the good Lord invented fireplaces."

Inside, Daisy was greeted by a crackling fire and a living room so elegant she thought they might've stepped into the wrong home. Though the plaster walls were still cracked and the ceiling still riddled with holes, a sumptuous round area rug had been set in front of the hearth. On top of the rug was a burgundy velvet sofa with a Victorian flavor, but a hundred times more comfortable. Side tables held dancing candles and chocolates and cakes and pies and tarts.

Pressing her hands to her cheeks, Daisy confessed, "I—I don't even know what to say. No one's ever done anything like this for me. It's off-the-charts romantic." As was usually the case when her emotions got the better of her, Daisy began to cry, but this time, happiness was to blame.

"Hey..." Luke used the pads of his thumbs to brush

her tears away. "There's no crying when a guy's trying to get lucky."

"Oh—for creating this work of art, you're guaranteed a home run." She kissed him, then kissed him again and again.

"Would you be surprised if I admitted to having a little help from Josie and Wren?"

Nibbling a chocolate-covered strawberry, she said, "I'd be more shocked if you hadn't."

"Hey," he complained, "was that a dig at my decorating skills?"

"Not at all, sweetheart." She pressed a kiss to his lips. "Not at all."

This time when they made love, it was a leisurely exploration, enhanced by the shared knowledge that they finally had all the time in the world to share.

When Luke entered her, there was no pain, only rippling fissions of pleasure. "I love you," he said, using one hand to cup her cheek. "I wanted to tell you last time, but I was scared."

"You're not now?" Daisy needed to know.

Luke said, "I'm one-hundred-percent convinced marrying is what we need to do."

From then on, sensation became more important than conversation. Building need consumed her until she was too desperate to think. Their kisses grew ever more intense, deepened with chocolate-flavored sweeps of their tongues. When release finally came in a thousand shimmering waves of pleasure, Daisy cried out.

She'd never dreamed life could be so perfect. And she'd never loved a person more. Yes, Kolt was her world, but letting Luke in had only expanded that world, making it brighter and stronger and infinitely better for her and her son.

AN HOUR LATER, LUKE SAT on the sofa holding Daisy in his arms. The fire and candles may have burned down, but his feelings for her had only grown. "We're going to have an amazing life," he said, toying with a strand of her hair.

"Agreed. You don't mind moving in here, though, do you?"

"I'd be miffed if I didn't get to. It's going to be a great house. My mom's going to sprout green envy horns when she sees this place decked out for the holidays."

"Lucky for her," Daisy said, "it could be next year before we're open for holiday business."

"True," Luke said with a resigned nod. There were a daunting number of tasks left to do, but he had a feeling working together would make the jobs fun. Sure, they'd have their squabbles over paint colors and bathroom tiles, but overall, he couldn't wait to start their shared lives.

"Speaking of your mom, did you ever bring up the fight I had with her?"

"Yeah. I would like her to apologize, but she's sticking to her guns."

Easing upright, Daisy's eyes narrowed. "In what regard?"

"Look." He straightened as well. "There's no pleasant way to put this, so I'm going to come right out with it.

Mom and Dad feel I should take legal action to make sure Kolt's mine—you know, on paper."

"Whoa." Hands on her hips, she stood. "You're kidding, right?"

"No. They're dead serious. And it got me thinking—maybe they're right? I know you're not running again, but what could it hurt to put it in writing? Something along the lines of a formal prenup arrangement should you ever decide Weed Gulch isn't the place you want to be."

The last thing Luke had intended was to upset Daisy with his suggestion, but judging by her scowl, she was more than a smidge miffed, although dressed as she was—in her panties and his white dress shirt—it was hard taking her seriously.

"Aw, baby," he said, cinching his arms around her waist. "Don't be mad. Forget I ever mentioned it."

She laughed, but the sound was brittle. "How am I supposed to forget a thing like my future husband having so little faith that I'll stick around that he actually wants me to sign over legal rights to our son—just in case."

"Daisy, I didn't mean it like that." Or had he? Luke would be lying if he said a small part of him wasn't still gun-shy when it came to Daisy sticking around. She'd hurt him once so badly. Who was to say she wouldn't do it again? He hoped like hell she wouldn't, but the doubt remained all the same.

In the process of tugging his shirt over her head, she ruined her fancy hairdo. With her hair spilling at crazy angles, she was back to looking like the teenage girl he'd first loved. The same girl who'd first broken his heart.

She plucked her bra from the floor, putting it on with little fanfare before wriggling into her dress. Adding her heels, she began blowing out candles. "Would you please douse the fire. I know the chimney sweep said it was safe, but I don't want it burning when no one's home."

"Why are you doing this?" Luke asked, refusing to do one lick of her bidding until she came to her senses. "Considering the fact that I didn't even know I had a son until ten freaking years after his birth, is it really too much to ask for you to give me insurance in an ironclad, legal-type document you'll be sure to understand?"

"You won't put out the fire," she said. "Fine. I'll do it myself." Marching into the kitchen, she filled the bucket she used for cleaning. Her heels made a racket on the wood floors, the sound echoing through the empty house. With water on the flames, the logs hissed and smoked. She grabbed her coat, making quick work of slipping it on. "Ready?"

"You can't be serious?" he asked along with a sarcastic chuckle. "After all I did to make this night perfect, you're going to ruin it by pitching a hissy fit?"

"Oh—" Yanking off the ring he'd spent hours figuring out how to order online, she took his hand, setting the still-warm platinum band in his palm. "I've gone way past hissy into the realm of blind fury. The sooner you get me home, the better."

"You are home." Hoping words of reason might help her find her apparently lost sanity, he said, "Our home. You and me, remember? We just made love on the living-room floor. A second time on *our* new sofa.

Are you really going to give up what we share all be-cause I need black-and-white proof you'll never leave me again?"

"Yes," she said, voice hollow and cold, "because in the same respect, I need proof that the man I plan to marry trusts me."

DAISY SPENT THE REMAINDER of the night crying into her bedroom pillows. Thankfully, by the time Luke dropped her at home, everyone in her nosy family was either asleep or, as in the case of her son, engrossed in a movie that had far too many wall-shaking explosions.

How could Luke do this to her? To their son?

Was this a sign that she should chuck it all and return to San Francisco?

Her life had been so much simpler there. Work and Kolt had been her only two concerns. Yes, they'd also been her only loves, but in light of what had just trans-pired between her and Luke, it wasn't as though she had anything to salvage in Weed Gulch.

Her bedroom door creaked open, and just like old times, in marched her big brother, Dallas. "What's with the boo-hooing? After all the work me and a bunch of other guys did, don't tell me Luke botched his proposal?"

She shook her head and sniffled.

"What's the problem, then? I saw the ring and the guy's got style."

Rolling over to face Dallas, who sat down on the side of her bed, Daisy said, "H-he did give me his ring, and it was the best I've ever seen. The night was magic until he—" Still reeling from the shock of Luke's request, her tears started anew.

"Quit crying and tell me what happened." Dallas had never been the sappy, overly-emotional type.

After giving her brother the highlights reel on what had ranked right up there as the worst night of her life, Daisy asked, "Now, do you see why I'm so frustrated?"

Sighing, he looked to the ceiling, then back to her. "In a word, no. Now, before you go getting bent out of shape, let me explain. I've known Luke a hell of a long time and he's a good man, Daisy. He wouldn't have asked this of you unless he was scared. In all the times you two have been together, it's always been you walking away. Yes, this time I know you mean for your relationship to last forever, but can't you understand that from Luke's point of view, there's no such thing? This document he's asked for should mean nothing to you—because if you truly never intend to vanish again, you don't have to worry about losing Kolt." Squeezing her toes, he added, "Way I see it, it's a slam dunk for all three of you."

DAISY WOKE THE NEXT MORNING with Dallas's words still ringing in her head. She dropped Kolt off for school, and then drove straight to her office. She busied herself reading over a few documents for Barb. She helped a couple with a newborn to write wills. Most of all, she wondered if Dallas was right in that she was taking Luke's request far too personally.

Yes, it hurt to her core that he could make such a demand, but considering what she'd put him through, wasn't providing him with this relatively small measure of reassurance the least she could do?

For the next hour, Daisy wrote the most solid, binding child-custody agreement she could. When she finished, she emailed it to a friend who specialized in family law. Once Ally announced that the document was airtight, Daisy took her coat from a brass peg on the wall and set out to retrieve both her man and her ring.

Her throat tightened when she got to Luke's cabin and found his Jeep and camper were gone. Knowing Dallas cared for Luke's horses when he was out of town, she tracked down her brother who reported that Luke had left that morning for a job in Wyoming.

"How long's he going to be?" Daisy asked Dallas.

He sat at his desk, paying bills, and he was in no mood to chat. "I don't know. He was hoping for only a week, but in his line of work, he never knows. He'd turned it down so he wouldn't be away so close to Christmas, but once you ran the poor guy's heart through a meat grinder, he figured he might as well get back out on the road to start paying off your ring. Oh—and he wanted me to ask you to keep Kolt near a phone once he gets home from school."

Determined to see her mission through to a satisfying conclusion, Daisy wrangled from Dallas the route Luke would be taking, as well as his final destination. Next, she packed small bags for herself and her son. She kissed her mom, explaining exactly where she was going and what she planned to do. If there was anything she'd learned from her fight with Luke, it was always to be open with the people you love. Last stop was Kolt's school where she explained to his teacher that they were taking an educational field trip to see his father working. Armed with Kolt and enough schoolwork to keep him busy for over a week, Daisy was finally ready to go.

Would Luke be ready to accept her latest apology?

WRESTLING WITH A biting champion breeding mare in sub-zero wind cold enough to freeze spit, Luke figured he might've been better off staying home. On the flip side, his current company was a damned sight more logical than Daisy, whose tantrum still chapped his hide.

What had she been thinking, breaking up with him yet again? They worked together. Sure, they bickered, but half the fun of that was in making up.

His cell rang—not that he heard it over the howling wind, but he felt the vibration in his back pocket. Seeing the caller was his mom, he considered not answering but then decided to pick up. "Hey, Mom. I'm busy."

"So am I," she said. "But listen, I ran into Cami Vettle—the elementary school secretary—and honey, I don't know how to say this in a way that won't sting, but Daisy checked Kolt out of school for an indefinite amount of time and even gathered enough of his books and homework to last the rest of the year."

The tuna sandwich Luke had eaten for lunch threatened to come up. "You sure?"

"Marty down at the gas station said Daisy not only filled her tank, but bought an atlas. Now, I ask you, why would a woman with her means do that unless she was planning a trip?"

"I don't know," he snapped. Where the hell was Daisy

going with his son? Should he call Dallas? Alert him his sister was on the run again?

"Don't get angry with me," Peggy barked right back. "I'm just confirming what I knew all along. Daisy Buckhorn is no good."

Disconnecting his mother, Luke returned the mare to her stall. In this weather, she was too agitated to listen and he was too keyed up to speak.

His camper rocked in the wind as if he'd parked in the middle of a lake. Still, he put in a call to Dallas. When it went straight to voice mail, Luke truly started to panic.

"Mom," Kolt said, munching a sweet-smelling apple, "I'm pretty sure you just made a wrong turn."

Daisy argued, "But the GPS lady said this is the way."

Her oh-so-wise child sighed. "I'm telling you, she's wrong. We've learned all about maps in school and I think we should turn."

"Okay," Daisy said, "but it's cold and windy and we haven't seen any sign of civilization for an hour. If we have to spend the night out here, I'm eating all of your pretzels."

He laughed. "I know I'm right."

"You excited to see your dad?"

Nodding, he said, "I'm real glad you guys are getting married. It'll be fun having him live with us all the time. Plus, I've been meaning to tell you, I want an extra-big wedding cake."

Worrying her lower lip, she said, "Slow down, sweetie.

We don't know for sure yet if Luke even wants to marry me. Last time I saw him, I made him pretty mad."

Kolt said, "Don't worry, Mom. I know Dad loves you."

"How?"

"Because every time he talks about you, he gets a funny look on his face. Kind of the same way Jonah does when he's around Nancy Meir. I think she's gross, but Jonah's all the time talking about her shiny hair."

"That's a very bad sign," Daisy said, afraid to hope her son's assessment of Luke might be right. After two days on the road, more than anything she wanted Luke to give her one more chance. She knew she didn't deserve it, but she figured it never hurt to pray.

HAND TO HIS FOREHEAD, shielding his eyes from the worst of the dust the wind had kicked up, Luke eyed the car approaching the Triple C's barn.

No way…

Sure enough, Daisy's prissy gold Mercedes—dirty as ever, bucked over the potholed dirt lane. Seated in the front seat alongside her was Kolt.

Tears stung Luke's eyes, but he didn't even bother sweeping them away. His mom hadn't just been wrong, but acting downright senile. Daisy hadn't been running from him, but to him.

Chest swelling with hope that she'd tracked him down for a happy reason, he damn near stopped breathing when he noticed her expression as she left the car wasn't all smiles.

"Dad!" Kolt bolted from his seat, barreling himself against Luke for a man-size hug. "I missed you."

Kissing the top of his son's head, Luke said, "I missed you, too, bud."

"Did you miss Mom?" Kolt asked.

Luke didn't have a quick answer. Yes, he'd missed her so bad he hadn't even wanted to eat. But his logical side kept reminding him that he'd survived ten years without Daisy. Surely he could go a few more.

"It's all right if you didn't," Daisy said. She wore faded jeans, sneakers and a ratty University of Oklahoma sweatshirt Luke recognized as belonging to Dallas. In her hands she carried a legal folder she struggled to keep steady in the wind. "That said, in the event you did miss me—want to see me again—I took the liberty of drawing up this."

"What is it?" Luke asked. Had she written the legal papers he'd wanted? It seemed a bit silly now. A piece of paper proving trust. When his mom had told him Daisy had left Weed Gulch, Luke's first instinct had been to panic, but a quiet voice of reason reminded him to stay strong. Daisy had grown, so had he. She wouldn't hurt him again.

"I want you legally to have equal custody of our son. As his father, you could easily enough obtain it on your own, but I wanted it to come from me. This, too." She handed over a small pouch, containing a folded document.

"First, come inside," he said, putting his arm around both of them, guiding them to his trailer.

"This is cool!" Kolt said, bouncing on the bed. "Can I come horse-whisper with you?"

"Sure," Luke said, all the while never dropping Daisy's gaze.

"Now that we're out of the weather," she said with a shiver, "have a look. I—I think you'll like it."

A quick scan of the document inside showed it to be his son's birth certificate. Daisy Buckhorn was listed as Kolt's mother and Luke Montgomery as his father. Luke's throat ached from holding back tears. "All this time? But I thought you'd listed his father as unknown."

"You *thought* it," she said. "During one of our hundred arguments I was going to tell you, but got interrupted. I'm done hiding things from you, Luke. You'll never know how sorry I am for hurting you. You have to understand that no matter what, I want to make decisions that affect both of our lives as a team. If your offer's still good, I don't want to be Daisy Buckhorn anymore, but Daisy Montgomery."

"Am I gonna be Kolt Montgomery?" their son asked.

"Yes," Daisy said, "no matter what. I've already filed the paperwork."

"I love you," Luke said, too relieved for words. Not about the custody agreement. He knew he didn't really need it. He was relieved that he and Daisy and Kolt were finally going to be a family. "Your ring's at my cabin, but once you get it back on your finger, I'd better not ever see it off."

"Yes, sir." She sealed her promise with a kiss.

"Why don't I get a ring?" Kolt asked.

"Because you're getting a custom-built tree fort," Luke said. "I already had a friend of mine draw up plans, and just as soon as your mom's carpenters finish her jobs, I'm putting them to work on ours."

"I love you, Dad." Kolt squeezed Luke in a hug.

His throat tight with emotion, Luke said, "I love you both."

"Hey," Kolt pushed free. "There's only one of me."

Daisy and Luke laughed.

"I was talking about your mom," Luke noted, "but if you want to leave her out of our fort, I suppose we can have a special vote."

"Nah." Kolt gave his mom a hug, too. "I love her, too, but Jonah says if you get married, Mom's gonna have a baby and if she smells as bad as Mabel and Robin when they poop, then I don't want her coming anywhere near our fort."

"Agreed," Luke said. "But what if your mom has a boy baby?"

Kolt took a moment to ponder this. "I s'pose then it would be okay. Boy babies don't smell as bad, do they?"

Cupping her belly, Daisy's eyes sparkled. "There's only one way to find out."

* * * * *

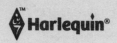

Harlequin®

COMING NEXT MONTH

Available July 12, 2011

#1361 THE TEXAN AND THE COWGIRL
American Romance's Men of the West
Victoria Chancellor

#1362 THE COWBOY'S BONUS BABY
Callahan Cowboys
Tina Leonard

#1363 HER COWBOY DADDY
Texas Legacies: The McCabes
Cathy Gillen Thacker

#1364 THE BULL RIDER'S SECRET
Rodeo Rebels
Marin Thomas

You can find more information on upcoming
Harlequin® titles, free excerpts and more at
www.HarlequinInsideRomance.com.

REQUEST YOUR FREE BOOKS!
2 FREE NOVELS PLUS 2 FREE GIFTS!

LOVE, HOME & HAPPINESS

YES! Please send me 2 FREE Harlequin American Romance® novels and my 2 FREE gifts (gifts are worth about $10). After receiving them, if I don't wish to receive any more books, I can return the shipping statement marked "cancel." If I don't cancel, I will receive 4 brand-new novels every month and be billed just $4.24 per book in the U.S. or $4.99 per book in Canada. That's a saving of at least 15% off the cover price! It's quite a bargain! Shipping and handling is just 50¢ per book in the U.S. and 75¢ per book in Canada.* I understand that accepting the 2 free books and gifts places me under no obligation to buy anything. I can always return a shipment and cancel at any time. Even if I never buy another book, the two free books and gifts are mine to keep forever.

154/354 HDN FDKS

Name	(PLEASE PRINT)

Address	Apt. #

City	State/Prov.	Zip/Postal Code

Signature (if under 18, a parent or guardian must sign)

Mail to the **Reader Service:**
IN U.S.A.: P.O. Box 1867, Buffalo, NY 14240-1867
IN CANADA: P.O. Box 609, Fort Erie, Ontario L2A 5X3

Not valid for current subscribers to Harlequin American Romance books.

Want to try two free books from another line?
Call 1-800-873-8635 or visit www.ReaderService.com.

* Terms and prices subject to change without notice. Prices do not include applicable taxes. Sales tax applicable in N.Y. Canadian residents will be charged applicable taxes. Offer not valid in Quebec. This offer is limited to one order per household. All orders subject to credit approval. Credit or debit balances in a customer's account(s) may be offset by any other outstanding balance owed by or to the customer. Please allow 4 to 6 weeks for delivery. Offer available while quantities last.

Your Privacy—The Reader Service is committed to protecting your privacy. Our Privacy Policy is available online at www.ReaderService.com or upon request from the Reader Service.

We make a portion of our mailing list available to reputable third parties that offer products we believe may interest you. If you prefer that we not exchange your name with third parties, or if you wish to clarify or modify your communication preferences, please visit us at www.ReaderService.com/consumerschoice or write to us at Reader Service Preference Service, P.O. Box 9062, Buffalo, NY 14269. Include your complete name and address.

USA TODAY *bestselling author B.J. Daniels*
takes you on a trip to Whitehorse, Montana,
and the Chisholm Cattle Company.

RUSTLED

Available July 2011 from Harlequin Intrigue.

As the dust settled, Dawson got his first good look at the rustler. A pair of big Montana sky-blue eyes glared up at him from a face framed by blond curls.

A woman rustler?

"You have to let me go," she hollered as the roar of the stampeding cattle died off in the distance.

"So you can finish stealing my cattle? I don't think so." Dawson jerked the woman to her feet.

She reached for the gun strapped to her hip hidden under her long barn jacket.

He grabbed the weapon before she could, his eyes narrowing as he assessed her. "How many others are there?" he demanded, grabbing a fistful of her jacket. "I think you'd better start talking before I tear into you."

She tried to fight him off, but he was on to her tricks and pinned her to the ground. He was suddenly aware of the soft curves beneath the jean jacket she wore under her coat.

"You have to listen to me." She ground out the words from between her gritted teeth. "You have to let me go. If you don't they will come back for me and they will kill you. There are too many of them for you to fight off alone. You won't stand a chance and I don't want your blood on my hands."

"I'm touched by your concern for me. Especially after you just tried to pull a gun on me."

"I wasn't going to shoot you."

Dawson hauled her to her feet and walked her the rest of the way to his horse. Reaching into his saddlebag, he pulled out a length of rope.

"You can't tie me up."

He pulled her hands behind her back and began to tie her wrists together.

"If you let me go, I can keep them from coming back," she said. "You have my word." She let out an unladylike curse. "I'm just trying to save your sorry neck."

"And I'm just going after my cattle."

"Don't you mean your boss's cattle?"

"Those cattle are mine."

"*You're* a Chisholm?"

"Dawson Chisholm. And you are…?"

"Everyone calls me Jinx."

He chuckled. "I can see why."

*Bronco busting, falling in love…it's all in a day's work.
Look for the rest of their story in*

RUSTLED

*Available July 2011 from Harlequin Intrigue
wherever books are sold.*

SPECIAL EDITION

Life, Love and Family

THE TEXANS ARE COMING!

Reader-favorite miniseries Montana Mavericks
is back in Special Edition with new loves,
adventures and more.

July 2011 features *USA TODAY* bestselling author
CHRISTINE RIMMER
with
RESISTING MR. TALL, DARK & TEXAN.

A Texas oil mogul arrives in Thunder Canyon on
business and soon falls for his personal assistant. Only
one problem—she's just resigned to open a bakery!
Can he convince her to stay on—as his bride?

Find out in July!

Look for a new
Montana Mavericks: The Texans Are Coming **title**
in each of these months

August	September	October
November	December	

Available wherever books are sold.

www.Harlequin.com